F. A. Paley, W. M. Fawcett

A Manual of Gothic Moldings

SALZWASSER
VERLAG

F. A. Paley, W. M. Fawcett

A Manual of Gothic Moldings

1st Edition | ISBN: 978-3-75258-679-4

Place of Publication: Frankfurt am Main, Germany

Year of Publication: 2022

Salzwasser Verlag GmbH, Germany.

Reprint of the original, first published in 1865.

A

MANUAL OF GOTHIC MOLDINGS.

A MANUAL

OF

GOTHIC MOLDINGS:

WITH

DIRECTIONS FOR COPYING THEM AND FOR DETERMINING THEIR DATES.

Illustrated by upwards of Six Hundred Examples.

BY F. A. PALEY, M.A.,

AUTHOR OF "A MANUAL OF GOTHIC ARCHITECTURE," ETC.

THIRD EDITION, WITH NUMEROUS ADDITIONS AND IMPROVEMENTS,

BY W. M. FAWCETT, M.A.,

JESUS COLLEGE, CAMBRIDGE; ARCHITECT.

LONDON

M.DCCC.LXV.

EDITOR'S PREFACE—THIRD EDITION.

A Third Edition of the Manual of Gothic Moldings having been called for, the present Editor, at the request of Mr. Paley, has undertaken to prepare it for the Press. Though it is always difficult for one person to carry out satisfactorily the work of another, the Author was of opinion that the revision of a professional man would secure accuracy, and give the work that practical character which he wished it to have.

The additions and alterations that have been made, have chiefly been done by way of further explanation where anything might not previously have seemed clear to a student; at the same time, the Editor has been careful to keep the book within its present limits, lest he should change its whole character from an elementary treatise to one of an entirely different class.

A considerable number of woodcuts have also been inserted by way of additional illustration, and, as far as practicable, the localities of the examples in the plates have been indexed; but, as these were taken from the Author's note-books when the work was first published, many of them cannot now be ascertained with certainty.

The Author has employed the terms "Early English," "Decorated," and "Perpendicular" throughout, and these are so thoroughly engrafted into the work, and are, besides, so generally understood, that the Editor felt it would have been undesirable to attempt any alteration. But the student should remember that the object to be attained in nomenclature is to define clearly the date and locality at which certain kinds of work prevailed. Now the two latter of these terms do not fulfil this condition, and therefore, in using them, the student must be careful that he knows the dates to which they refer. Several new terms have been proposed, but those here employed have become so generally adopted that no others have succeeded in displacing them. Mr. Fergusson has proposed the adoption of Edwardian and Plantagenet in a manner analogous to Tudor, Elizabethan, &c., already in common use; also such terms as "early thirteenth century," "late fourteenth," &c., are frequently employed, and have the advantage of being very precise.

An accurate knowledge of Moldings is indispensable to any one professing even an amateur's acquaintance with architecture; but he who attempts to practise as an architect (however freely he may use his knowledge) must study them thoroughly, not merely by reading a work like this (though that may be of great assistance), but by actually going about observing and measuring them himself; for very little can be learnt without measuring, as *scale* has a very important effect on the character of Moldings.

There is, perhaps, hardly an old Church existing without something worth sketching in it; and often, in Moldings, charming little variations may be found, which at first sight would hardly be suspected. The Editor, therefore, feels that he cannot do better than advise those who wish to attain a true knowledge of the science of Gothic Moldings, not merely to read about them, but to sketch them carefully, and to measure them accurately.

CAMBRIDGE, 1st *December*, 1864.

CONTENTS.

A MANUAL OF GOTHIC MOLDINGS.

SECTION I.

INTRODUCTORY.

No person can have devoted much time and pains to the investigation of Christian architecture, as it was practised in this country during the Middle Ages, without feeling the importance of acquiring an accurate knowledge of MOLDINGS.* That certain conventional forms or details were in use at certain periods, and were uniformly adopted in the constructive decoration of all edifices, ecclesiastical and secular, throughout the length and breadth of the land, with varieties rather of combination or disposition than of the component members, is an undoubted fact, well known to and admitted by all who have paid any attention to the subject. But whence these forms arose, whether from a natural process of gradual development, or from some real or pretended secret of freemasonry, or, lastly, from mere accident or caprice, are curious questions, which, so far as the author is aware, have never yet been made the subjects of much investigation. Again, how far the same forms were arbitrary or obligatory in ancient freemasonwork, how far they emanated from some particular source, and were dispensed by authority through the country, or were assumed by some tacit agreement on the part of the masons themselves, are

* This, the ancient orthography of the word, has been adopted after Professor Willis.

equally interesting speculations, though, perhaps, equally difficult to determine. However this may have been, it is quite certain that a strict intercourse must have been kept up between the members of this body of artisans, or almost every ancient church would exhibit new and strange varieties in the details of its moldings. When the difficulty which then existed of constant and speedy communication between distant parts of the country is considered, this general resemblance and uniformity, not only indeed in moldings, but in all the parts and features of Church architecture, must appear still more surprising. There is in all these enough of licence and variety to give scope for occasional localisms, and to make it probable that each architect worked, to a certain extent, independently, and yet there is such resemblance and decided adherence to rule, as to make it evident that some *system* must have been observed both in designing and executing them.

Or can this acknowledged uniformity be referred to no more recondite cause than *fashion?* Can it be said, that as the same kind of hat, or coat, or other article of dress, is seen in London which is found in common use at York, with varieties, indeed, and a considerable degree of caprice in adorning or diversifying them; and that, as all these things are exclusively in the hands of certain bodies, as hatters and tailors, and no one ever dreams of employing others than these in providing them; so there was at once a fashion and a monopoly in architecture; and a solecism in moldings would have seemed to the ancient churchmen as striking and offensive a fault as a solecism in dress is now considered? Perhaps this is the most rational and probable view; but then it is one so very different from modern architectural practice, in which every professor is at liberty to design just as he pleases, and even when he pretends to imitate, is apt very freely to indulge his own pleasure, and even to ridicule the restraints of strict rule, that it certainly does appear strange and unaccountable.

However, all these questions are quite foreign to the object of the present work. They are all the province of the antiquary rather than the architect, and as such it is out of place to say anything more about them, especially as the writer is incompetent to give any solution of the difficulty which they involve. But this may reasonably be observed, that it is to be regretted that so little has yet been done in reducing to a science this interesting and practically important department of Gothic architecture. Probably a fancied uncertainty and obscurity of the study, or a want of sufficient data, or ignorance of the exact periods at which buildings were erected, and the apparent anomalies and inconsistencies which seem often to occur, have all tended to deter even the most competent from writing a complete treatise on the subject. To these may be added the tediousness of making any considerable collection of drawings and sections of moldings, the delay and difficulty of copying them with minute accuracy, and the amount of observation and research necessary for attaining a knowledge of their history and true theory. These are causes at once sufficient to render a first attempt imperfect, and to induce the reader to pardon any errors or deficiencies which he may notice in the course of the present work.

It may possibly be said, Why should such profitless pains be taken in investigating these dull and insignificant minutiæ: why should they not be copied in our new churches without writing books about them, and so turning an amusing pursuit into a hard lesson, by imposing on beginners so much to learn? The answer is, that moldings are of the greatest possible importance: so much so, that they have rightly been called "the very grammar of the art." They are by far the most certain, and very frequently the only guides in determining the dates of buildings, or of architectural members; they are just as essential to a knowledge of architecture, as a map is to the study of geography. In practice, too, they are of the first importance.

No one has any claim to the name of architect who thinks the science of moldings beneath his notice.

It must be confessed, that some years ago, on the first revival of the true principles of Gothic architecture, very serious, and indeed surprising mistakes were frequently committed, even by architects of repute, in the details of their moldings. There was but little discrimination of styles, and a general poverty of appearance prevailed, especially in the working of capitals and bases. In structures of that period even of considerable pretension it was but too common to find the most wretched and meagre imitations of ancient examples, the spirit and character of which were completely lost or perverted by some violation of leading principles.* It is gratifying to find such rapid improvement and so much increased attention on the part of our present architects, who are fully sensible of the great importance of correct moldings to the effect, as well as to the distinctive character of their designs.

A work on moldings may have any one of the three following ends in view. It may either contain a great collection of the best examples, accurately reduced to a scale, or accompanied by measurements, so as to form a magazine of reference, and thus supply the wants of practical men, who may often be unable to procure in their immediate neighbourhood any available models; or, secondly, it may profess to be a complete and elaborate exposition of the *theory* of moldings, dealing with principles rather than with bare facts, and taking a comprehensive view of the whole subject through the medium of the Classic and Romanesque varieties; or, lastly, it may be an elementary treatise, intended only to convey plain and easy information on the most ordinary forms, and on the differences observable in each style.

* As an instance, the molding of the rich and costly archway in the centre of the cloister to the new buildings of St. John's College, Cambridge, is partly Early English and partly debased Perpendicular; apparently an original composition of the late Mr. Rickman's.

The first could perhaps be satisfactorily accomplished only by a professional man, who might be supposed to know the wants of architects and the best method of supplying them. The second would require not only very considerable acuteness and ingenuity, but the observation and collections of many years. The last alone seems capable of being tolerably well treated by an amateur, who has himself seen the want of some work on the subject, and been thrown entirely upon his own resources in examining and investigating it.

Such then is the aim and object of the present work, of which the method of treatment is simple and practical as far as possible. It is obvious that the number of examples given might be absolutely unlimited, and that to attempt a complete illustration would require many hundreds of engravings, and a judicious selection out of thousands of drawings. Such extensive resources the author does not profess to possess; nor can he even assert that every one of the examples he has given, from a collection of a few hundreds of full-sized sections, and about as many drawings, made at different times and places by the eye alone, is of that perfect and minute accuracy which might have been obtained by a laborious reduction of full-sized outlines to one and the same scale. The object being to explain details and formations, and to point out differences, rather than to furnish models for modern imitation, this extreme faithfulness of delineation, though of course highly desirable, is unnecessary, and was in the present case quite impracticable. For the same reason the measurements are only occasionally added.* The specimens engraved are mostly those of ordinary occurrence, rather than examples of rare exceptions to the general practice of the ancient architects.

Viewed as an inductive science, the study of Gothic moldings is as curious and interesting in itself as it is important in its

* Most of the woodcuts, and the examples in the last five plates, have been reduced from actual measurements.

results. Any one who engages actively in it will be amply repaid, if only by the enlarged views he will acquire of the ancient principles of effect, arrangement, and composition. The curves, the shadows, and the blending forms, are really in themselves extremely beautiful, and will soon become the favourites of a familiar eye: though, viewed without understanding, they may seem only an unmeaning cluster of hollows, nooks, and shapeless excrescences. Many persons are not aware that every group can be analysed with perfect ease and certainty; that every member is cut by rule, and arranged by certain laws of combination. But such is surely the case; and a knowledge of the fact should convince the student of the reasonableness of the study. Let him only enter upon it, and he will be rewarded for his pains. The only necessary conditions are, a tolerable idea of delineation, and a general interest in Church architecture. Possessed of these simple qualifications, he will be led on by his subject from step to step, almost imperceptibly, ever observing and adding to his store of facts and examples, and tracing out to his own satisfaction the forms and processes through which he conceives moldings to have passed in the various stages of their development. He will learn to pronounce with confidence the date of the merest fragment of sculptured stone. A broken piece of a capital, a string-course, or a door-jamb, dug up on the reputed site of an ancient building, will tell him of what style and date the fabric was, of which so insignificant a remnant alone remains.* He will ever

* The Messrs. Brandon have pointed out the interesting fact, that although earlier styles were occasionally imitated in completing or altering buildings at a later period, the moldings of the respective eras were always most faithfully preserved. "The assimilating process never extended to the *moldings*. To however great an extent the earlier portion of an edifice may have been subsequently copied, these important members were always worked in strict conformity with the ordinary system prevalent at the time of their construction."—Analysis of Gothic Architecture, p. 10, Introduction.

and anon meet with some new and singular conformation, perhaps overturning his previously formed theories, — perhaps clearly reducible to and confirmatory of them. He will look at every ancient building, however dilapidated or defaced, with a more searching eye,—for he will be sure to find in its very demolition peculiar facilities for research. He will regard every shattered arch with a new attention. He will find the same satisfaction in examining it (a melancholy satisfaction perhaps, yet a like feeling of keen interest) which a botanist finds in a rare plant, a herald in an ancient escutcheon, or a geologist in an undescribed fossil.

The learner must be duly apprised that the best work on Gothic moldings which could possibly be written will do no more than set him in the right way to obtain a knowledge of the subject by his own research. A few examples in the page of a book are as nothing, if he does not apply in practice that which he has learned from them. The look of a molding is so very different in section, projected in a reduced size on paper, from its appearance in perspective reality, that the same form seen in the one may not even be recognised in the other. It is here, therefore, once for all explained how the engravings are to be understood.

Supposing a molded archway were to be taken down, and any one of the voussoirs or arch-stones placed upon a large square sheet of paper, in such a manner that the *wall-line*, or part of the stone which lies in the plane of the outer wall, should be parallel with the end of the paper nearest to you, and the *soffit* or inner surface, at right angles with it, parallel to one side; and then a pencil were to be carried along the wall-line first, and afterwards in and out of each cavity and round each projection, and so up a portion of the soffit-plane; the outline thus obtained reduced to a small size (say a scale of half an inch to a foot), and shaded on the part which represents the flat side or bed of the stone, would form a diagram exactly similar to our illustrations. Again, if a string-course were to be sawn across, or a capital or base down the middle, and a piece of paper inserted in the crevice, and marked off by the sharp edge of the molding, this would in the same way represent the shaded sections of these details. The usual *popular* way of engraving Gothic moldings is to give a perspective sketch of a stone or slice cut out of the arch, showing at once the flat end or upper face, and the molded side, and shading the cavities and projections, as in the woodcut and PL. V. fig. 5. But this, though its general appearance is certainly much more like the reality, does not give so clear a view of the *forms* of the separate members. The method adopted by architects is uniformly that which has been followed in the plates illustrating the present work. Each example is, in fact, the same as the *templet* or *mold*, a thin plate of zinc, tin, or wood, which is used by workmen in marking out the stones previously to cutting them out. The shaded portion of PL. XII. fig. 15, is a good illustration of a templet.

Decorated door-jamb, Maxey, Northampton.

But the student must not only *observe;* he must *copy* moldings in order to understand them. Without the latter, his knowledge will never be practically perfect. How to do this, will shortly be shown, by explaining some of the various methods which have been practised. It must be understood, at the outset, that though certain lines, planes, and measurements may be drawn in all cases to assist the process, and ensure general fidelity, they are somewhat difficult to copy accurately by the eye, because the exact curves, which are not always geometric, can scarcely be caught without considerable practice. And if the true form is not attained by the first stroke, the endeavours to improve it will seldom be very successful. Perhaps the student's first attempts will be altogether futile; but it is surprising how well and how readily a *practised* hand can copy in a few minutes a most complex group. A small note-book should be kept exclusively for copying moldings by the eye, the measurements and name of place being duly registered with each example.*

For the medieval nomenclature of moldings, the learned and useful work lately published by Professor Willis, and already alluded to,† supplies an authentic source of information. In this treatise, some of the ancient names of moldings have been recovered; and it is to be hoped they will be revived, especially in the present dearth of terms.

A few expressions used in the present work it will be necessary clearly to define before entering upon the subject.

Any architectural member is said to be *molded,* when the edge or surface of it presents continuous lines of alternate projections and recesses.

A drawing which represents these lines as they appear to the eye placed exactly opposite to them, is called the *elevation* of a molding, as in PL. I. fig. 8; PL. X. figs. 1 to 5, 22, 24, 40.

A drawing which represents the outline of these projections and recesses, is called the *section* or *profile* of a molding, being the appearance it would present if cut through *by a plane at right angles to its bearing.* Thus, PL. I. fig. 10, if cut across A B, would present the appearance of fig. 5.

A *mold,* or molding (the former is the ancient term), commonly signifies the entire series which ornaments a jamb or arch; but it is here generally used in the sense of a particular part or member of such series.

Members are said to be *grouped,* when placed in combination, as we generally find them; but

* Nothing is better adapted for a pedestrian tourist than a *block* sketching book, in the pocket of which a small "T square," for ruling parallel and rectangular lines, should be kept. These are to be obtained with the leaves fixed on one side, so that they form a book when complete, and the objection to having a number of loose sheets is obviated.

† The Architectural Nomenclature of the Middle Ages, being Part IX. of the Transactions of the Cambridge Antiquarian Society.

A *group* is a bunch of moldings or separate members, standing prominent or isolated, either on a shaft or between two deep hollows.

An arch of two or more *orders*, is one which is recessed by so many successive planes or retiring sub-arches, each placed behind and beneath the next before it, reckoning from the outer wall-line. Thus, PL. I. fig. 5, is the section across an arch of "two orders," and fig. 7 is of "three hollow-chamfered orders."

As it is necessary for every student in this science, first to understand the general principles of formation, and, secondly, to be able to draw or "take" moldings, either full-sized or reduced to a scale, with tolerable precision, these preliminary points will be explained as simply and briefly as possible, before entering upon the consideration of the combinations and more minute varieties of detail.

SECTION II.

THE GENERAL PRINCIPLES OF FORMATION.

It seems certain that all the forms of Gothic Moldings are the peculiar and genuine offspring of Christian architecture, or at least are very partially and indirectly borrowed from the Classic styles; although, as might be expected, some coincidences of form exist between them. There are some who contend that Gothic moldings are derived, mediately indeed, yet very decidedly, from Roman; a supposition hardly probable in itself, when we observe that in the Norman style (in England at least), which was most closely connected with the Classic, the forms of the moldings which we call Gothic are merely nascent, and entirely undeveloped; and one which appears scarcely tenable, from the consideration that the medieval architects of this country* could have known little of Italian architecture, and if they had, we cannot suppose they would have cared to copy in its details what they altogether repudiated in its kind. But the convincing argument is this: that in Gothic molding all the links in the process of formation are connected and complete, from the first and rudest origin to the most elaborate development; and the steps are so natural, the transitions so easy, that any two styles working independently of each other from the same beginnings and elemental forms, could hardly fail of arriving at least at some of the same results. Again, if at this or that period a new member was introduced, and, as it were, a new letter added to the alphabet, why should it not be attributed to invention, rather than sought for in the resemblance which an Italian molding may happen to bear to it? However, the discussion of this question is rather for those who have to do with the theory of moldings, as the determination of it does not in the least affect the facts of which this work treats.

From the time of the formation of the first Christian Basilica to the middle of the twelfth century, there is such a general resemblance in the character of the work as to have caused it to be classed under the one title of Romanesque. About that time it must be remembered that the whole of Western Europe was engaged in the first Crusade, and though it can hardly be said that the early Gothic forms are mere copies of Classic or Eastern ones, the effect of travel would naturally be to ac-

* It is true that the Freemasons were an ecclesiastical body under the Pope, and not confined to this or any other particular country in Europe. It is also true that the intercourse with Rome was always frequent, from the time of St. Augustine downwards. Still it is impossible to trace in pure Gothic buildings the least symptom of Italianizing either in composition or details. This view the writer is happy to be able to confirm by the coincident opinion of the authors of the Analysis of Gothic Architecture, page 48.

custom the mind to see beauty in an entirely different class of forms, and to enlarge its capacity of designing according to the requirements it met with.

That the whole tone of architecture was then altered is an undoubted fact, and some leading features were then introduced for the first time. Also in matters of mere detail, we find new forms, some of which may be traced to foreign sources: the Early English base is allowed by all to have been borrowed from the Attic; and it will hereafter clearly be demonstrated that such was the case. And it is undeniable that several forms and combinations of the ogee curve are nearly identical in Classic and in Gothic buildings. Still, if every Gothic form can be shown to be an improvement or modification of a preceding one, it must be concluded that the whole series is the offspring of one and the same progressive art.

In their use also Gothic moldings differ as widely as possible from Classic. The former are repeated to almost any extent, so as entirely to occupy the large recessed spaces in jambs and arches. They are repeated too in groups, each group being composed of the same members, or nearly so, especially in the earlier styles. The latter are few in number, and very limited in their application. The combinations of the one are in a great measure arbitrary, though the forms themselves are fixed; in the latter both are absolutely defined. The former run principally in vertical lines, the latter in horizontal. In Gothic architecture, horizontal moldings occur in water-tables and string-courses, and in capitals and bases, in which positions they invariably form subordinate lines, so as to contrast and display the predominant principles of a vertical ascending sweep, and may so far perhaps be regarded as lingering vestiges of the Classic usage—evidences of the victory of Christian over Pagan art. For it is needless to remind the reader that Gothic owes its origin, though not its development, to the Basilican, that is, to Roman architecture.

An intelligent and thoughtful writer in the *English Review* * has the following remarks on the differences between Grecian and Gothic moldings: "Where the Grecian delighted in broad level surfaces, catching the light in masses, or in projecting curves on which it dies away by degrees into shadow, the Gothic roughened and encrusted them with carving. And thus in general we measure, or, if the expression may be used, we read and peruse, a Grecian molding by its lights, and the Gothic by its shadows." Again: "Of the differences between the two classes of molding, some may be detected by a superficial view. For instance, the Grecian delights in convex lines, the Gothic in concave; the Grecian in broad lights, the Gothic in narrow. The Grecian throws out projections to catch the eye; the Gothic endeavours to bury it in deep recesses. The Grecian leads it gently along in sweeping, unbroken undulations; the Gothic fractures its lines, and combines them in angles and curves. The lights and shadows of the Grecian melt and slide insensibly into each other; those of the Gothic are planted together in strong and bold contrast. . . . . . In the purest Grecian buildings, vertical moldings are rare. Horizontal moldings form the leading lines; and it is by these, even in later and degenerated specimens, that the vertical moldings are regulated. In the Gothic, vertical moldings are most frequent; and they overrule and determine those which are horizontal. And Grecian moldings are simple and easily divisible into parts; Gothic are entangled in labyrinths, and perplexed with innumerable intricacies."

The notion of ascending moldings is coeval with the introduction of the arch, and may indeed be traced to a still earlier period in the sides of doorways and similar positions. When the Romans broke up, by means of the arch, the continuous horizontal entablature of the Grecians, the cornice moldings were carried around it, and fell on each side in vertical lines into

* For December, 1844.

the horizontal, thereby producing the same result as in Gothic, though with a different effect; in the one case, horizontal lines continuing to predominate, in the other, being subdued and rendered secondary and subordinate to the vertical principle.

Gothic architecture revelled in the use of moldings, not only what are usually called *ornamental* moldings, such as the dog-tooth, the ball-flower, &c., but also the plain continuous lines of light and shadow; though they are in effect identical, since the former are nothing but serrated ridges,* more or less rounded and modified from the first process. Every door, window, monial,† every edge, vertical or horizontal, every band, string, groin-rib, roof, label, arch, and jamb, whether of wood or stone, internal or external, was generally molded. Of course the effect produced by so free and extended a use of them was magnificent in the extreme. Construction gained thereby a rich perspective, a depth of shade, an attempering of bare prominent outlines, a fine tone, which arrested the eye, and made it dwell on certain parts of higher pretension and more exquisite elaboration than others. And yet moldings are merely the ornamental adjuncts, not the essentials, of architecture. Some buildings of the best periods were quite devoid of moldings; whence it is evident that they are not necessary even to a perfect design. Boldness and simplicity produce effects, different indeed in their kind, yet not less solemn and striking than richness of detail. But the power of moldings was appreciated to the full by the ancient architects, and it is quite evident that they delighted in their extensive use. It was their ambition to work them wherever they could possibly find means and opportunity. Hence it is that such a vast quantity every-

* This may occasionally be seen, when the molding was left for some reason or accident partially uncut. It is probable that they were generally worked out after the completion of a building.

† The medieval term for what we now call *mullion*.

where remains, that no ordinary pains are requisite in examining any considerable moiety of them for the purposes of investigating their principles. If the uniformity in their use had not been very strict and close, it had indeed been a hopeless task ever to master the subject; indeed, if there had not been a *system* of molding, there would have been nothing to investigate. But so little did the medieval masons depart from the fixed conventional forms, that a capital, a base, or an arch-mold is often found of perfectly the same profile in an abbey or a cathedral, and in a village church at the other end of the kingdom; so that we might almost suspect that the very same working drawing had been used for both. And this, when it is considered, must appear a very wonderful fact.

Although the examples given here are in nearly every case from stonework, the student would do well to notice those in other materials, such as wood, iron, &c., for though the same forms will be found at the same date as in stonework, they are on a more delicate scale, according to the fineness of the material; thus, in the annexed examples, the monial from the screen at Burgh le Marsh, Lincolnshire, is only half the size of the stone one from Bottisham, near Cambridge, but has more members in it.

Woodwork, Burgh.

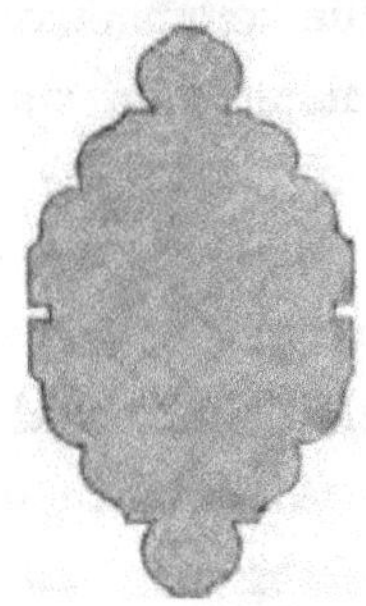

Stonework, Bottisham.

The reader will perhaps be tired of this preliminary chapter, and will be anxious to enter upon the subject at once. And at this point it may be well to proceed, beginning with very early buildings, and endeavouring to discover the origin of the practice, and then gradually trace the progress of development until the forms have all been analysed and classified according to their respective dates.

On examining the plan of a Saxon window or door-way, perhaps nothing more will be found than a rude square-edged aperture in a plain wall, as in PL. I. fig. 1. This may often be met with, even considerably later, in small and rude country churches, especially in belfry-arches. It may, however, be relieved and expanded by splaying it on one or both sides, that is, by sloping or chamfering off the edges, as in fig. 2. So in an ordinary Early English lancet window, the long narrow opening has a very wide splay inside and a very small one on the outside, fig. 3. But in arching over the upper part of such an aperture as fig. 1, made in a thick wall of loose rubble masonry, it was not uncommon to add, for the sake at once of ornament and security, a sub-arch, or under-rib, like the groin-rib of a vault, constructed of fine-jointed ashlar, as fig. 4. This sub-arch rested either on a pillar at each side, or a projecting impost,* or it was carried continuously down to the ground, that is, without any interruption or change of shape. Now in this rude arrangement, which is observable in many continental Romanesque churches, and may probably be connected in its origin with the overlapping stone courses or *fasciæ* in Classic architraves, we shall find the germs of a usage which ever afterwards prevailed, with some improvements of form and detail, but no alteration of principle. In the abbey church of St. Alban's, the nave and transept-arches are constructed of two rectangular sub-ribs, or soffit-pilasters, which are continued from the ground with the intervention of a mere band or string-course at the impost. The same is observable in several of the Transition arches at Buildwas Abbey.†

By chamfering off each *arris*, or square edge, of this aperture, which now becomes *recessed*, or of two *orders* or retiring members, the plan is at once obtained which was most con-

* In Transition arches, the inner order, or sub-arch, is often corbelled off at the impost, the jambs being left square, with a small shaft at the angles.

† Potter's Monastic Remains, PL. III. and IV.

stantly used, especially in pier-arches, without the least change of form, for centuries afterwards (PL. I. fig. 5). Of course, there may be two or more sub-arches, if the wall be very thick; each one retiring behind the other. And the chamfer may be hollow, or fluted, as in fig. 7, which is common in Early English and Decorated arches. This is the case in the chancel-arch at Cherry Hinton, near Cambridge, and was much in vogue from about 1260 to 1320.

In practice, however, when worked on a small scale, the sub-arch was no longer a separate constructive formation, but was cut out of a single stone together with the first or outer order of moldings. The accompanying diagram represents a voussoir or arch-stone of an ordinary Decorated nave-arch.

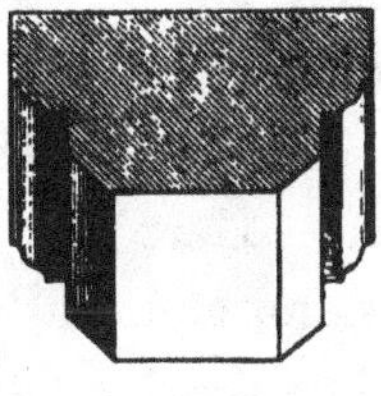

It is quite evident that the above was the origin of the commonly occurring arch of two plain chamfered orders. Were any proof wanting, we might refer to cases where only one side is chamfered and the other left square, as at Horningsea, near Cambridge, circa 1190 (PL. I. fig. 9), or to the peculiar termination represented in elevation in PL. I. fig. 10, and PL. XXI. fig. 3, which is common in Early English arches, as at Waterbeach, near Cambridge, or to the springing of a three-quarter edge-roll from a square archivolt immediately above the capital, as in PL. I. fig. 8, which is a Transition Norman arch at Little Casterton, Rutland. Fig. 10 may conveniently be called the *broach stop*.* It is the way of changing the square into the chamfered edge without abruptness, or of blending the one into the other.

But there was another method of taking off sharp edges, which was introduced perhaps even earlier than the other, and exercised a much more direct influence in the formation of

* The broaches of an octagonal spire are the semi-pyramidal projections connecting the four oblique faces with the angles of the square tower.

moldings. This was by rounding the edge instead of cutting it away. Hence arose the cylindrical roll or BOWTELL, which was afterwards made more or less nearly a circle by cutting out a small angular channel on each side. PL. I. fig. 6, is one side or face of an arch-mold at Little Casterton, showing this method, which is given more at large in fig. 21. This seems soon to have suggested the contrast of light and shade, formed by hollows alternating with (relatively) projecting members.

Fig. 11 is the section of a Norman pier-arch at Friesland, Lincolnshire. In this the square edge is worked into a shallow triple roll.

Fig. 12 is an Early English pier-arch at Skirbeck, near Boston. Here the bowtell is formed by rounding the edge as before, and cutting a deep three-quarter hollow on each side. Thus the bowtell becomes attached only by a narrow neck, as was very usual in this style.

Fig. 13 is from Great Grimsby, and fig. 14 from Clee, both in Lincolnshire. In the latter church a Dedication inscription still remains,* bearing the date 1192; and the other is of very nearly the same period. Both these are good examples of the same principle; and arch-molds of this kind are of constant occurrence in the Norman and Transition styles. The pier-arches in the nave of Peterborough Cathedral are molded precisely in the same manner.

These bold early moldings are generally called "edge-rolls," because they occur at the external angles of the receding orders, and are not yet extended on each side. They are commonly single, as PL. XXI. fig. 2, an arch from Seaton church, Rutland; but occasionally double, as fig. 1 of the same plate, the belfry arch of Morcot church, in the same county. From this latter arrangement is derived the double roll and fillet which forms the central member of PL. XVIII. fig. 8, an arch-mold from the choir of Ripon Minster.

* Facsimile given in Rickman's Gothic Architecture, Sixth Edition, p. 234.

In considering the origin of the cylindrical roll or bowtell, the first element of moldings, the influence of jamb-shafts, must be taken into account. In Norman doorways, every nook formed by the receding under-ribs, already described, is occupied by a detached column. PL. I. fig. 15, is from Adel Church,* Yorkshire, and illustrates this arrangement. Now this column seems at first to have borne a square-edged member or sub-arch, which projected above the impost exactly where the jamb receded below it, and which was afterwards, in some cases, rounded off so as to correspond in form and size with the column itself. This may very clearly be seen in an Early Norman doorway at Hauxton, near Cambridge. Hence, by omitting altogether the impost or capital, the idea of continuous moldings is obtained. This subject, however, will be spoken of more fully in treating of capitals and shafts generally.

Another form, which occurs frequently in the Transition Norman and Early English periods, is the POINTED BOWTELL, resembling, and coeval with, the introduction of the pointed arch. Its formation may be seen in PL. I. fig. 16, which is the plan of a late Norman arch in St. Mary's Church, Ely. This member arose from a desire to decorate the angles of recessed arches, without either cutting away or rounding off the square edge, as in the annexed example from Croxden Abbey, Staffordshire. Hence its occurrence in Early Gothic may be expected,

and in truth it is very frequently found in the Transition period, though not in the pure Norman. Yet something closely resembling this member often occurs in Norman work, between two cylindrical bowtells, as at A, fig. 13. Fig. 17 is a triple respond or half-pier, of very singular form, at Clee; and

* See "Churches of Yorkshire," Part VII., from which this example is borrowed.

fig. 19 shows its use in an Early English arch at St. Benet's, Lincoln. In this case the under-edge is withdrawn at the point, which seems the origin of what is called the *scroll-molding,* hereafter to be explained. Fig. 24 shows this form more at large.

The pointed shaft, the plan of which may be described as a spherical triangle engaged at the base, is of constant occurrence in Early English work, and is generally a mark of its early date. The clustered columns at Byland and Whitby Abbeys (the former circa 1190) exhibit the pointed shaft alternating with the circular. The western porch at Ely is flanked by clustered columns of pointed shafts. Undoubtedly this form existed earlier than, and afterwards led to, the filleted shaft and bowtell, which are so well known by the name of the "roll-and-fillet." As a general rule it may be stated that a shaft may take almost any form to suit the primary molding which it sustains on its capital, on the principle of continuous moldings already alluded to.

PL. I. figs. 12 and 23 show the cylindrical and the pointed bowtells with the addition of a small fillet at one side. Fig. 22 is a groin-rib from Robertsbridge Abbey, where both sides are thus filleted. Fig. 18 is a groin-rib from Tintern Abbey, where the fillet is at the end or central point. And fig. 25 is an Early English arch at Little Casterton, where there are three fillets. Of all these varieties more will be said hereafter.

PL. II. fig. 1, is a pier-arch of very Early English date, at Middle Rasen. Fig. 2 is a doorway at Ludborough, fig. 3 the chancel arch at Langtoft, and fig. 5 the jamb of the archway of the south porch at Great Grimsby, all in Lincolnshire. The first three exhibit the use of the pointed bowtell. PL. XVIII. fig. 4, is the jamb of a lancet window at the east end of Rivaulx Abbey. This is one of the commonest moldings at the angles of Early English window-jambs.

The student will already have perceived, from the manner

adopted here of drawing the sections, first, that all these moldings are *formed out of the solid block solely by removing edges and sinking hollows*, and must never be regarded as excrescences on a plane surface; secondly, and in consequence, that *the groups lie in the planes of the uncut blocks*, the outermost edge of each member touching the rectangular or chamfered surface, that is, not being cut away so as to fall below or short of it. The original planes, or uncut square surfaces, are represented in our engravings by dotted lines. These two facts must be regarded as fundamental canons in the arrangement of moldings.

There are three planes in which moldings will be found to lie; one parallel with the outer wall, which we shall designate the *wall-plane;* one at right angles to it, or parallel with the soffit, which may be called the *soffit-plane;* and the third, the plane formed by chamfering an edge, which was generally (not invariably) done at *an angle of about forty-five degrees* or the *chamfer-plane.* In PL. II. fig. 10, A is the chamfer-plane, B the soffit-plane, C the wall-plane. It is clear that by sinking hollows in any one of these surfaces, a group of moldings would be developed.

In considering any series of moldings previously to copying them, the first point is to lay down on paper the various planes, that is, to ascertain the plan of the arch, or other feature, before the moldings were cut. When this is done by accurate measurement, the rest of the process becomes comparatively easy, and the most complex and extensive combination, which it appears at first sight impossible to copy with anything like accuracy, may be readily disentangled, analysed, and sketched with precision. Without attending to these facts, all attempts to do so will be futile.

It may be alleged, as a general rule,* that Early English

* "In the Anglo-Norman style the jamb-molds were almost always worked in the wall and soffit planes; and this continued to be the general

moldings lie on the planes rectangular; that Decorated, according to their kind, fall either on these, or on the chamfer-plane alone; and that Perpendicular moldings almost always lie on the last. If some members seem to fall short of one plane, they will generally be found referable to some other; and if they fall on the segment of a circle, which is much more rarely the case, as in PL. II. fig. 15, a pier-arch at All Saints', Stamford, the inclination must be determined by bending a ruler or piece of lead across them. It is, however, by no means uncommon to meet with moldings of all the styles in which some of the members are withdrawn considerably below the plane of the others. It is obvious that this is the most expensive kind of molding, because more has to be cut away from the solid block. The arrangement of moldings on the original block-planes was less and less rigidly adhered to as the styles progressed, and in the latest, or Third-pointed, it was frequently entirely lost. PL. III. figs. 2 and 3, are instances of Early English moldings not falling upon the regular planes.

PL. II. fig. 11, is an example of a molding from Over, Cambridgeshire, truly copied according to the above rules. Fig. 12 is the distorted and inaccurate form it would probably assume if an unpractised and untaught draughtsman were to attempt to copy it by the eye.

PL. II. fig. 7, is an Early English molding from the interior of the chancel door, Cherry Hinton. Fig. 8 is a pier-arch, and fig. 6 the northern doorway of the same church. Fig. 19 is a very fine molding from the inner door of the south porch.

arrangement throughout the Early English Gothic period, although we occasionally find the jamb molded on the chamfer-plane. During the earlier portion of the Decorated Gothic period, the wall and soffit planes still continued to be most generally used, but then in tolerably frequent connection with the chamfer-plane, which at this time was in most cases worked exactly at an angle of 45°; and as the style advanced towards the era of decided architectural debasement, the moldings shared in the prevailing desire to produce a meretricious effect, without any reference to correctness of composition."—Brandon's Analysis, p. 50.

(The semicircle round the central group represents the capital of the jamb-shaft.) Fig. 9 is a doorway, and fig. 13 a window-jamb, both from Over. These are Early Decorated. Fig. 14 is a doorway at Madingley, and fig. 16 one at Trumpington, near Cambridge. These are both pure Decorated. Fig. 18 is a magnificent arch-mold from the doorway of St. Clement's church, Cambridge, showing the capitals of the two jamb-shafts. This is not an easy example to copy by the eye, for the central member in each group does not extend to the angle, but falls on the line of the chamfer. The observation of this circumstance immediately removes the principal difficulty.

This section illustrates a very common peculiarity of its style, which may be called the *triplicity* of moldings. Whether constructive or symbolical, or (as a writer in the *English Review*, already quoted, imagines) suggested by philosophical principles of effect, we need not now consider, though symbolism may have had its influence, since the architects of the period greatly affected representations of the mystic number THREE. This molding consists of three distinct groups, each group having three members. Occasionally each member has three fillets, so that there is a *triple triplicity* in the entire composition. It is clear, however, that if an archway has two sub-arches, or consists of three orders, the angle of each will naturally form a group of three rolls with a hollow on each side, as in fig. 5. Early English and Decorated moldings very often consist of three groups. Too much stress has frequently been laid on the theory of architectural symbolism, and we only mention it as an opinion entertained by some.

SECTION III.

OF COPYING MOLDINGS.

THERE are several ways of doing this. The best and simplest of all is by inserting the paper in a loose joint, or by applying a large sheet of paper where a stone has been removed, and left the edges sufficiently clear and sharp to trace their outlines by pressure against them, or by a pencil. These methods, however, are but seldom available, except in ruined buildings, and here great care should be taken not to damage or destroy any portion of the little that is left. But many fragments of monials, groin-ribs, voussoirs, and other molded stones, may be found in every old abbey; and these may readily be placed upon sheets of paper for the purpose of tracing their outlines. By these means alone a large collection of very valuable specimens may be made.

Another way is by the use of the leaden tape. A thin flexible riband of this metal, about a yard in length, may be rolled into a coil so as to be easily portable. By being manipulated and impressed upon the moldings to be copied, and thence carefully removed, and laid upon a sheet of paper, it retains the exact shape it has received, and may be traced off with a pencil. In this process, however, which requires both pains and practice to ensure tolerable accuracy, there are many difficulties to overcome. First, it is clear, that if the molding extends over a considerable space, the tape, by its extreme pliability and great weight, is almost unavoidably bent in transferring it to the paper, which must be spread flat on the ground, or some level surface nearest at hand. If this should happen, the true bearings of the members, that is, their relative position to each other, are confused or altogether lost, and the copy is incorrect and worthless. Secondly, where the molding is much undercut, or contains deep and wide hollows with a narrow neck, the lead, when fitted into them cannot be withdrawn. In the first instance, it is better to copy only eight or ten inches of the molding at once; or the planes in which the members respectively lie (that is, a full-sized plan by measurement of the block jamb or arch) may be first marked out on the paper, and the tape adjusted to them; in the second case, it is advisable to carry the tape merely over the necks of the hollows, and subsequently to determine their breadth and width by inserting a measure into them. As Early English moldings are often mutilated, from being so far undercut that portions of the projecting members have fallen or been broken off, the lead may frequently be manipulated into a part which is entire, and afterwards drawn upwards or downwards till it finds exit at a broken place. In all cases, dirt, moss, and whitewash must first be scraped clear away from the part to be copied, or the sharp and rounded edges, the depth of the hollows, &c., cannot truly be ascertained.

In using the tape, the rough draught of the pencil must invariably be corrected by close comparison with the original, and every separate member should be tested as to size, projection, bearing, and curvature, by the aid of the measure. A pair of compasses with the ends bent inward is very useful in obtaining the breadth of the members; and if furnished with a segmental scale-bar, or slide affixed to one leg and passing through the other, the width of the neck of each undercut bowtell may be exactly marked. Sharp edges and angular hollows cannot be closely copied with the leaden tape, so that these especially must be supplied by the eye; on the whole, though the tape has in some cases been successfully used, it is so clumsy that it can hardly be recommended to the student.

There is a process similar in its nature and results to the use of the leaden tape, which is very successful where the moldings are not too much undercut. This is technically called *squeezing*, and is practised by applying wet clay, plaster, or a composition purposely prepared of wax and some other ingredients, to the part to be copied, the form of which is thus readily and accurately obtained, though the convex and concave surfaces are of course reversed. By pouring plaster of Paris into the matrix thus formed, the original molding is exactly copied. But in the case of undercutting, the difficulty is here insurmountable, and the whole operation is tedious, clumsy, and only fit to be applied when a *model* is necessary.

A beautiful and ingenious instrument has been invented by Professor Willis, and called by him the Cymagraph, by which moldings may be copied with the most perfect accuracy, and of the full size. It is described and illustrated in the *Engineers' and Architects' Journal*, No. 58. It can be successfully used with a very little practice; and the most extensive and complex moldings can be taken by its aid. The only disadvantages are, that the instrument, though by no means large, is an inconvenient appendage to the equipment of a pedestrian, and that only about a foot's width of a molding can be taken at once; so that a number of separate pieces of paper must be pinned together on the spot, and that with great accuracy, or the planes and bearings will be incorrect.

Another instrument of great elegance, and about the same size, has (since the first edition of this work) been brought to a considerable degree of practical utility, though not perhaps fully to perfection, by Mr. Henry Bashforth, a Fellow of St. John's College, Cambridge. This very clever contrivance possesses the remarkable advantage of copying moldings on the spot, reduced to any scale which may be desired; and by reversing the process, the reduced copy may afterwards be enlarged to its original or any other size. In smaller and simpler moldings, as in ordinary door and window jambs, bases, and capitals, and the like, this machine answers perfectly, with one and the same application, as the author of the present work can attest, from having used it in company with the inventor; but for very extensive and deeply undercut groups, it is generally necessary to take a portion at a time, as in the case of Professor Willis's cymagraph.

Geometric methods, both of copying and reducing moldings, are fallible; for the members and curves were very often drawn *libera manu,** especially in earlier work; so that very considerable deviations from geometric precision must be expected in observing ancient examples.

Another, and for ordinary purposes much the best and simplest way, is to copy by the eye alone, on a reduced scale, adding the measurements of each face, as in PL. I. fig. 12. If the *particular* measurements of each member are required, they should be given in respect of a horizontal and a vertical plane, as in PL. II. figs. 20, 21, 22. This is rather a troublesome process, and is apt to produce a complex diagram. Generally, it is enough to give the whole breadth or width of a series of moldings, which is simple and easy when they lie in one plane, as in PL. III. fig. 1, an Early English doorway at Louth. The depth to which hollows are sunk from the surface of any plane may readily be added, as PL. VIII. fig. 3.

By adding the measurements of all the parts, any inaccuracy of proportion resulting from a hasty sketch will readily be rectified, should the molding be adopted in practical architecture. For example, in PL. XVII. fig. 3, it is obvious that the double groove or hollow chamfer in the centre cuts off a less portion of the projecting angle than the diagram represents; for the line marked 3¾ inches is nearly as long as that marked 7. In this, as in other cases, the measurement serves to correct the drawing.

For the sake of neatness, in copying moldings, it is well to

* If not so designed by the master, they certainly were often so cut by the mason. Mr. Potter, in giving the full-sized sections of mouldings from Tintern Abbey, has drawn them for the most part with the compasses, and in this case no doubt correctly.

adopt uniformly the plan, already pointed out, of drawing the outer wall-line parallel with the bottom of the page, and the soffit parallel to the side. The same side of a doorway or a capital should be taken in all cases where it is possible, to avoid the natural awkwardness of presenting to view the position of moldings drawn promiscuously right or left.

The practice of copying moldings by the eye alone, is of the greatest importance in acquiring a sound acquaintance with the subject. It is indeed, as before stated, *indispensable*. The eye becomes perfectly familiar with every kind and variety by frequently contemplating new examples and collections previously made; and thus a great degree of accuracy is in time attained, and a perfect copy of the ordinary and plainer moldings, with their measurements, may be made in two or three minutes. In this way also moldings which are quite out of reach may be sketched very tolerably at the distance of many feet, if the planes in which they lie be carefully attended to.

Though the student should always carry his sketch-book and pencil with him, he must be careful not to neglect to get full-sized details whenever he has the opportunity, as they will tend very much to correct the eye for sketching, and frequently show important deviations from geometric forms which are liable to be overlooked at first sight.

These two points, the planes in which moldings lie, and the relative proportions of the parts, must be invariably observed, and the practised eye will seize the outline almost instinctively, with a very close approximation to truth. It may be remarked, that in the example given by Professor Willis, in his "Architectural Nomenclature," from the Journal of William of Worcester, the plane is marked by a line, as in the illustrations of the present work.

In copying the moldings of capitals, measure the depth from the top of the abacus to the under side of the astragal, or neck; and the projection of the abacus over the shaft. Both these are easily taken by dropping a small plummet (a string with a

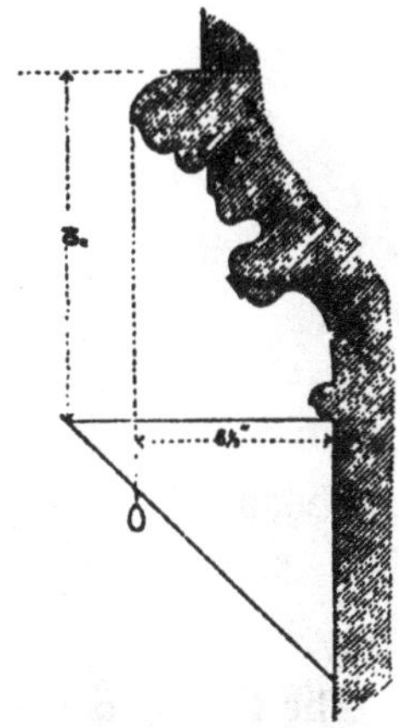

bullet is best) from the outer edge of the abacus, and applying the foot rule and triangle.

It has been observed that edges are frequently chamfered at an angle of forty-five degrees. But as this is by no means invariably the case, it is advisable in every instance to put it to the test. There are several simple and effective means of doing this. One is by bending the measure at its joint (PL. II. fig. 15), by which the angle can be accurately transferred to the paper, however small the copy may be: the only difficulty is in the hinge of the rule, which will prevent it being placed close against the wall. Another by the use of a triangle of wood or brass, with angles of forty-five degrees, by applying the hypotenuse of which to the chamfer the two sides will be respectively parallel to the wall-plane and the soffit-plane, if the chamfer is at an angle of forty-five, but not otherwise. See PL. V. fig. 12. The best plan, however, is to measure along the wall and soffit planes, which may generally be done very easily by placing the rule against one plane and sighting the end of it to a line with the other, as in diagram, where the rule is placed against one plane, the end just meeting the other, and thus either the dimension A B or B C may be obtained; and the enclosed angle being a right angle, the direction of the chamfer is obtained.

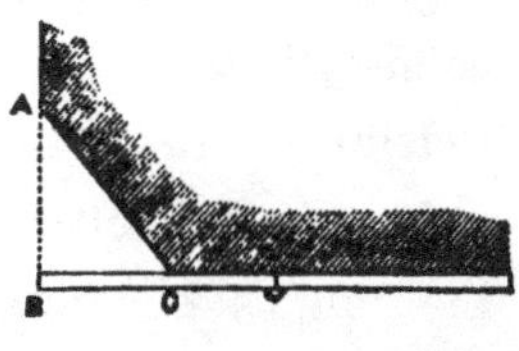

Full-sized moldings are reduced by the use of the well-known instrument called the Pentagraph. All other methods require both time and care. Every member may be reduced separately by means of the compass and scale; or circles may be drawn, inclosing certain portions of the copy, and repeated of the proportionate size in the same positions on the reduced drawing.

SECTION IV.

OF EARLY MOLDINGS IN GENERAL.

HAVING thus far explained the general principles and the methods of drawing moldings in section, the theory of the first formations of moldings must now be considered more fully.

The first and rudest attempts at molding which are found in this country, are the rough and coarsely chiselled members, generally semi-cylindrical, which occur in the Ante-Norman chancel-arch at Wittering, Northamptonshire, PL. III. fig. 10, the balustre shafts in the tower of St. Benet's, Cambridge, and other churches of that date, to which must be added the very curious and antique attempt at a molded architrave on the impost of the belfry-arch at Barnack. This last example, an exact parallel to which occurs in a doorway* of the Romanesque palace of Theodoric at Ravenna, and, indeed, the very nature of the case, would lead us to conclude that the earliest element arose out of a desire to relieve, by coarse irregular channeling, a plain flat surface. And a square-edged rib easily became a semi-cylindrical bowtell, by first chamfering, and then removing indefinitely the remaining angles. Thus, for instance, Norman string-courses often consist of a square projecting fillet, with the angles chamfered off, so as to form a semi-hexagonal projection. St. Sepulchre's church, Cambridge, affords, both in its groin-ribs and pier-arches, an excellent illustration of the first idea of forming rounds by removing edges, and of setting off the parts thus rounded, by sinking a small channel or furrow on each side a little below the surface. Thus, then, a square-edged arch, with its sub-arch or soffit-rib, was either

* Engraved in Mr. Gally Knight's "Italian Architecture," Part I.

worked into rounds at each angle, PL. IV. fig. 1, or into pointed rolls, as fig. 2, which is an arch at Reymerston, Norfolk, circa 1200; or some edges were chamfered, others worked into rolls, and the sub-arch cut away into a broad semi-cylindrical rib, as in fig. 4, which represents a semi-Norman arch at Barholme, Lincolnshire, and PL. XXI. fig. 1. PL. IV. figs. 7 and 8, are groin-ribs of common profile in Norman work; the one from Glastonbury, circa 1200; the other from Peterborough, Early Norman: both clearly and satisfactorily exhibiting the formation of the roll-molding or bowtell.

The deep rounded hollow (as contrasted with the mere notch), by which the contrast of light and shade was obtained, was an after-thought, which was not developed till the Early English period, when it was carried to an extravagant excess, so that roll-moldings were extensively undercut or attached only by a small neck of stone; thus having the effect of a series of detached arches or ribs, rising in succession above and behind each other, each independent and unconnected, the eye being unable to penetrate to the depth of the dark hollow. PL. IV. fig. 5, is a very Early English pier-arch, at Barnack, in which the first appearance of the deep hollows may be traced.*

It might appear probable that the true origin of the deep three-quarter circular hollow must be looked for in the wish to form a cutting *inwards*, at the point of the interior angle, corresponding to the bowtell at the edge or point of the exterior rectangle of the sub-arches, as in diagram and PL. VI. fig. 10, and PL. VII. fig. 7. From these two points both the hollows and the bowtells may have been extended each way, till no space was left unoccupied, and thus a great width was covered

* An excellent example of a similar kind is engraved in p. 85 of Professor Willis's "Canterbury," where the contrast between the Norman edge-mold and Transition bowtell with side hollows is well shown.

with minute members, alternately dark and light, hollow and prominent. Still, this inner hollow at the angle is not very observable in the earliest arches, but is rather characteristic of the work of the first two Edwards, so that this view is hardly correct.

The roll-molding being once established, it became natural to multiply it as an ornamental feature to an unlimited extent; and to prevent sameness of effect many modifications in the forms of the projecting members were introduced, as well as considerable variety in the size and depth of the alternating hollows. Now, multiplication naturally implies reduction in size; so that, in place of two or three heavy round moldings placed at the angles only, and without hollows of any great depth, we find a whole series of minute and skilfully diversified members, designed not on any exact geometric principle, but regulated by taste, effect, and no doubt, to a certain extent, by caprice. We may suppose the architect to have drawn on a board or a stone, with a free hand, the outline to be followed in working out the hollows; and PL. IV. fig. 3, represents such a stone, with the profile scratched or marked on its surface. The templet, being applied to every stone to be worked, afforded exactly the same shape for each, so that the pieces, when put together, coincided with perfect accuracy.

Deeply recessed archways consist of several courses of molded stones, each *order*, or sub-arch, having its own independent construction, and each joint being overlapped by the stone next to the back of it. When the moldings are meagre, the arch generally consists of a single row of voussoirs. In taking a molding of the former kind, it is well to mark the joints of the different courses.

The grouping and multiplying of members was greatly facilitated in its development by the Gothic principle of distributing weights and thrusts under a number of different supports. Thus each group of arch-moldings in an Early English doorway is borne by a detached jamb-shaft below the impost. In later times, the shafts were engaged in the wall, and at the latest period the roll-moldings were often continuous, but with small pseudo-capitals and bases attached after the manner of real columns.

The Norman architects never got much beyond the plain cylindrical edge-roll and shallow hollow, similar to the annexed example from Coton. They paid so much attention to surface sculpture and shallow ornamental work in the flat faces of their arches, that the notion of alternate hollows and projections does not appear to have been fully comprehended by them, or, if so, was found to be incompatible with the enrichment by shallow superficial detail. It was reserved for the period of Transition to effect this.

Coton.

The invention of the pointed bowtell, contemporaneously with the general use of the pointed arch, opened the way to a great number of new forms, all more or less referable to this common origin, and all used with the most refined taste in varying the members of complex Early English groupings. The first and by far the most important of these is the ROLL-AND-FILLET, PL. II. fig. 4, and PL. I. fig. 20, a doorway in the precinct of Lincoln Cathedral. The introduction of this new feature may be said to have wrought a complete revolution in the system of molding. It is the key-note of almost all the subsequent formations. It may be defined to be a flat bead set ribwise on the surface of a roll-molding, at first with a square under-edge, as PL. I. fig. 18, afterwards, and most commonly, with a slope or ogee curvature, as in PL. II. fig. 17, a groin-rib from Tintern Abbey. It is not certain at what precise period, or from what cause, the fillet was first added to the cylindrical bowtell. It was itself a common enough feature down from Classic times, and in Norman work was used in the abaci of capitals, in strings, and in other places. A certain analogy may be traced in the annexed examples; and that from Selby is simply the ordinary roll-and-fillet used as a string. An example of a single side fillet to the roll is figured PL. I. fig. 12. This appears to be an accidental one, being merely the uncut surface of the wall. Forms of this kind have probably first suggested the use of fillets with the roll. Or it may be that the idea of a surface-line having been suggested by the pointed bowtell, the fine feather edge was either cut off (PL. IV. fig. 9), or was throated or widened, so as to produce a more prominent effect. As, however, it will be found in the earliest examples that this fillet frequently falls in a line with the chamfer-plane, as in PL. II. figs. 9, 15, 19, and in fig. 6, the north doorway at Cherry Hinton, it may possibly have been left as a standing portion of the uncut surface; a view which is certainly borne out by the general analogy of molding. The position of diagonal projection is undoubtedly the ordinary one throughout the Early English period; and the fillet is not often found coincident with either of the other planes, as in fig. 8, a pier-arch from Cherry Hinton, till towards the end of the thirteenth century. Still, examples are not wanting in much earlier molding; so that it is not intended to insist on this theory of its origin.

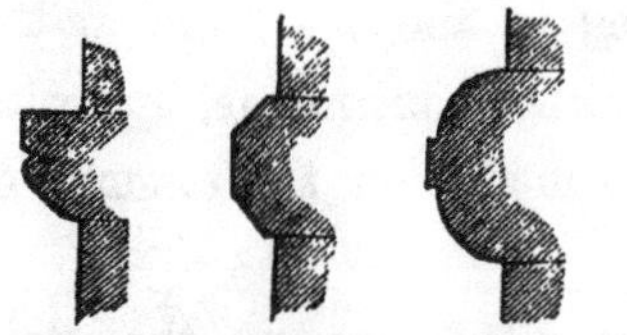

Ovolo and Fillet. St. Sepulchre's, Cambridge. Selby; String in Nave.

One fact is worthy of notice in the use of the roll-and-fillet; that it commonly occurs in alternation with the pointed bowtell; whence it would appear to be merely a variety of the latter, introduced for the sake of contrasting and diversifying the members of a group. For example, PL. II. fig. 5, has in the central group a filleted roll between two pointed ones. So also fig. 8; and the juxtaposition of these two forms may be noticed in many other instances.

Another plausible account of the origin of the roll-and-fillet may be offered. Its occurrence in early groin-ribs cannot have escaped the notice of the observer. Perhaps, indeed, the earliest instances of its use may be traced to the obvious propriety of forming sharp and hard edge-lines instead of mere round members in positions in which, from their distance, the eye would otherwise have an ill-defined and imperfect outline. Again, in *mitering*, or joining rolls at right angles, as well as in making them die into or spring out of plane surfaces, the addition of the fillet presents important advantages in neatness of construction.

But all these are mere conjectures. The author has devoted considerable pains and attention to the discovery of the true origin of this very important feature, but without satisfying himself with any of the theories given above, though the first seems the most probable.

SECTION V.

OF EARLY ENGLISH MOLDINGS.

FROM THE ACCESSION OF RICHARD I. TO DEATH OF HENRY III. A.D. 1189 TO 1272.

THE characteristics of the moldings of this style may be defined as deep undercut hollows between prominent members, which comprise a great variety of pointed and filleted bowtells, clustered, isolated, and repeated at certain intervals; a great depth or extent of molded surfaces; and the general arrangement in rectangular faces, as shown in PL. II. fig. 5. The hollows are seldom true circles; and, like the projecting parts, they assume a great number of capricious forms. PL. III. figs. 2

and 3, would alone be quite sufficient to convey to the eye an idea of the general method. The first is the belfry-arch at Plymouth, the second the pier-arches in the choir of Ely Cathedral. Both were taken with the cymagraph, and are reduced to a scale of half an inch to a foot.

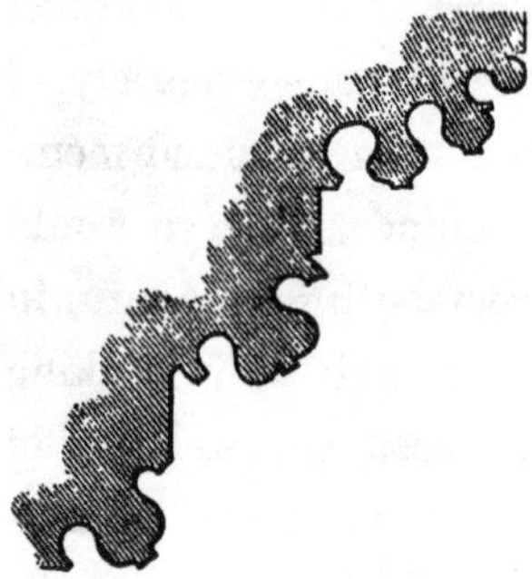

Early English Arch, Ripon Cathedral.

The annexed section will also serve as an illustration of the ordinary forms of Early English moldings.

Early English moldings may be said to comprise the following members :—

1. The plain bowtell or edge-roll.
2. The pointed bowtell.
3. The roll-and-fillet.
4. The scroll-molding (rare).
5. Angular forms, consisting of chamfered ridges and intervening projections, of irregular character.

The other forms chiefly consist of modifications of the roll-and-fillet, which are so capricious as almost to defy any attempt to assign them distinct names and formations. It will be right, therefore, briefly to point out some of the most commonly occurring varieties, leaving a more particular investigation to the student's own exertions.

The roll-and-triple-fillet (PL. I. fig. 25; PL. IV. fig. 3, A.) is much used in the more advanced buildings of the style, and was the favourite form during the reigns of the first two Edwards. The ordinary roll-and-fillet projecting from a ridge (PL. VI. fig. 5; PL. VII. fig. 12), each side of which is undercut by a deep hollow, naturally produces, and therefore probably suggested, this compound molding. It will be observed in PL. V. figs. 5, 6, 9; PL. VII. figs. 7, 8; PL. II. figs. 18 and 19. A plain bowtell or roll very often stands forward upon a short ridge or neck in Transition moldings, the edges being sharp on each side, in consequence of a slight hollow immediately below. This is of frequent occurrence even in semicircular arches, and may be found in doorways of that kind in many of our abbeys, as at Fountains. It is illustrated in p. 90 of Professor Willis's Canterbury (fig. 37, pier-arches of the choir). Sometimes only one side has a fillet attached (PL. I. figs. 12, 23). Sometimes there are two fillets, one at the top, the other on the side, as in the cut from Ripon, and PL. V. fig. 3, and PL. XVIII. fig. 1. PL. II. figs. 11 and 13, are varieties of very frequent occurrence. PL. IV. fig. 12, is a form often found in labels, as fig. 13, both from Lincoln Minster; the latter also illustrates the fillet as it were depressed into the roll. Fig. 11 is the chancel doorway at Ludborough, Lincolnshire, which shows some other varieties; in fact, the combination of the roll-and-fillet having been once suggested, they seem to have been used together with the utmost licence. Fig. 15 is a groin-rib from Furness Abbey. PL. III. figs. 4 and 7 are groin-ribs from Robertsbridge Abbey; 5 and 6 are fragments from Tintern and St. Mary's Abbey, York. Fig. 9 is the arch-mold of a double piscina with its capital from Histon, near Cambridge.

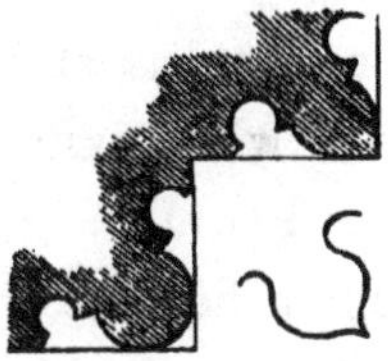
Doorway, Fountains Abbey.

Ripon Cathedral.

The members in PL. IV. fig. 11 fall wholly on the chamfer-plane, as in PL. III. fig. 1, which is seldom the case in this style. Three pointed rolls placed together, somewhat in the form of a fleur-de-lis,* form a combination of very frequent occurrence.

* There is sometimes so close a resemblance to the head of a fleur-de-lis in this complex molding, that it is difficult to disconnect the idea of the one from the other. An example is given, full size, in PL. XIII. of Potter's Monastic Remains, Tintern Abbey,—a work, we may here observe, which is quite invaluable in showing the curves and geometric formations

It may often be found between the detached shafts of large doorways, as at Peterborough and Ely, and indeed in any position, with many minor varieties of shape. PL. IV. fig. 21, and PL. II. fig. 5, are examples. In some cases it closely approaches the character of the roll-and-triple-fillet, as PL. V. fig. 6, the beautiful Decorated window-jamb at Northborough, Northamptonshire.

In Decorated work the fillet became extremely broad, PL. IV. fig. 19, often as much as three, or even four inches. In this case it may be said to lose its original character, especially in clustered piers, where it very often occurs, as in those to the east of the octagon at Ely. But in Early English it is almost always a narrow edge-line. If set square on the roll, it is generally a sign of early work. See the outline diagrams in PL. IV. The depressed and elongated forms on each side of fig. 11 are principally found in later buildings, the first in Decorated, the latter in Perpendicular.

It has been before stated that a great degree of licence is observable in the forms of Early English roll-and-fillet moldings, in respect of size, shape, and composition, and that geometric accuracy was avoided in a rather remarkable manner; the irregular shape, and the freely undulating curve, having been commonly preferred. Almost every conceivable modification of the plain roll, peaked, depressed, elliptical, grooved at the end, might be found and catalogued by a careful observer.

An important form, generally considered distinctive of Decorated, but not very uncommon in advanced Early English work,* is the SCROLL-MOLDING; so called from its resemblance to

of early moldings, and which every lover of Gothic architecture ought to possess. It contains an immense number of moldings of the finest era and the richest design.

* It occurs, for example, in the moldings of the very elaborate triplet at the east end of Castle Rising Church, PL. XVIII. fig. 6, engraved in PL. VIII. of Mr. Bowman's account of that church in his Specimens of Ecclesiastical Architecture. The presence of the scroll-molding in any

a roll of thick paper, the outer edge of which overlaps upon the side exposed to view. It may be described as a cylinder, the under half of which is withdrawn, or shifted a little behind the upper. It is almost universally used in the abacus and neck of Decorated capitals, and very often in strings and base-moldings.

It is certain that this form was known and in use even in the pure lancet architecture of 1200–1240. PL. I. fig. 19, from St. Benet's, Lincoln, is a proof of this. It also occurs, perhaps in an accidental or undeveloped form, in PL. II. fig. 3. It is represented in PL. IV., fig. 14, an Early Decorated doorway at Yaxley, Hunts, and in figs. 11 and 16,—the latter an arcade in Lincoln Minster. Here is seen the unusual combination of the scroll-molding and the side-fillet. PL. VII. fig. 5, is a fragment from Rivaulx Abbey. Fig. 7, the rich and beautifully moulded doorway at Northborough, circa A.D. 1270, exhibits the scroll form on the interior order.

Antiquaries are not agreed as to the origin of this molding. It may perhaps be regarded as a roll-and-fillet with one side left uncut, either because it was removed from sight, as in capitals, or afforded a more effective drip in strings and weatherings, where it most constantly occurs. The shadowed edge-line was presented by the scroll-molding as well as by the roll-and-fillet; and the principles of effect which suggested both forms are

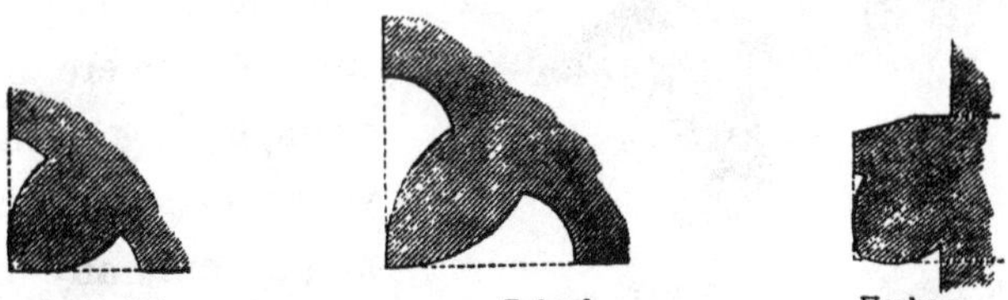

Roche Abbey. Byland. Hexham.

probably identical. But it is more probable that it was derived from the pointed bowtell. It may be traced from one form to

elaborate group marks its approach towards the Geometric age. See PL. XVII. fig. 6, which, together with the contiguous sections, figs. 4 and 9, represent the jambs of the immense Early Decorated and Geometric windows in the south aisle of Grantham Church.

the other through such gradual changes, as to leave but little doubt on the subject.

The earliest pointed bowtell was simply the new form of the pointed arch used as a molding (as at Roche and Byland), but this was soon modified by having a slight sinking close to the edge, so as to make it a little sharper, as in these examples from Barnwell and Ely. This form has been called the keel molding, from its likeness to the section of a ship showing the form of the keel. When worked in with more deeply cut moldings, it stood more isolated, with a long neck; and, probably from the combination of the two forms, we find it occasionally turning the edge to one side, as in PL. XVIII. figs. 1 and 10, from which we immediately obtain the form in fig. 6, which is a regular scroll-molding; and in this case it will be observed that it pairs off with a pointed bowtell.

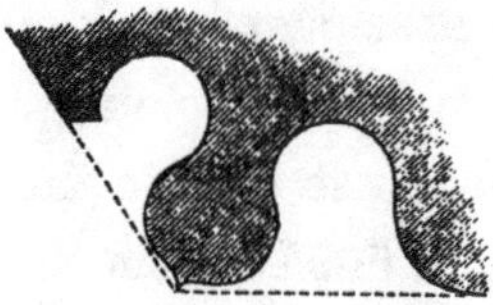

Barnwell, Cambridge.

Ely.

Rivaulx.

The annexed examples, also, from St. Mary's Abbey, York, and Tintern Abbey, show how closely allied the two forms are; and those in the choir arches of Rivaulx Abbey are an early example, in a position in which the pointed bowtell might naturally be expected.

St. Mary's, York.

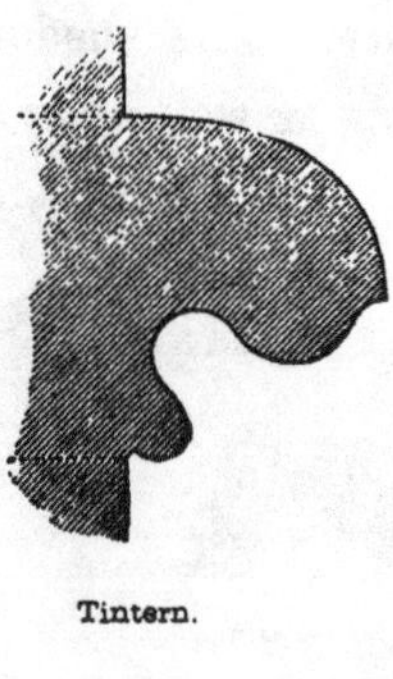

Tintern.

Though the under edge of the scroll-molding is usually rounded, it is frequently to be found cut square where sharpness of shadow was desired; but this can hardly be considered as a criterion of date, as it is to be found both in early work, as at Warmington, Northants, and down to the middle of the fourteenth century, as at Elsworth, near Cambridge. The scroll-edge is sometimes, though rarely, inverted, so that the withdrawn surface is placed uppermost, as in some of the bases at Tintern Abbey (PL. XIV. fig. 33).

Warmington, Northants. St. Michael's, Cambridge. Elsworth, Cambridge.

Two rolls-and-fillets conjoined at their bases, so that their respective fillets are at right angles to each other, constitute the DOUBLE-OGEE, or *double-ressant*, as it was anciently called,*—one of the commonest moldings of the Decorated and Perpendicular styles. It is rare in Early English, and apparently the result of accident rather than intention when it does occur, as in PL. IV. fig. 12. PL. VII. fig. 1, is the west doorway of Llandaff Cathedral, of pure Early English detail. The capitals which bear the two moldings in question are marked in outline. PL. IV. fig. 6, is a Decorated molding of sufficiently common occurrence (as in the belfry archway at Trumpington), where the shafts which carry the capitals are set together so as to form the double ogee. And the same may be constantly observed in the common arrangement of Early English and Decorated piers, PL. V. figs. 14 and 15. See also PL. II. fig. 17.

Early English arch-moldings are so easy to distinguish from all others, that it is not necessary either to say more in explanation of their peculiarities, or to give a great number of examples. They are by far the most difficult of all to copy with exactness, from the irregular and capricious forms of the curves and undercuttings; and their great extent, often many feet across, renders it an extremely tedious process to draw any

* Professor Willis says this molding is sometimes called *a brace*, from its resemblance to a printer's bracket. (History of Winchester Cathedral, p. 60, Proceedings of the Archæological Institute, 1845.)

of the rich and complex examples on a reduced scale. The numerous deep and dark hollows constitute the most characteristic difference between the moldings of this and those of the succeeding style, in which most of the forms already enumerated will be found to recur. But the extravagant display of deep cavernous undercutting is lost in Decorated moldings. We there find a hollow of three-quarters of a circle, accurately formed with the compasses, in the angle of every receding sub-arch, as in PL. VI. fig. 2, the west doorway at Hingham, Norfolk; fig. 11, the inner doorway of the south porch at Deopham; fig. 12, the same from Benington, Lincolnshire; and PL. XVII. fig. 3, from Bottisham, Cambridgeshire. And these hollows must be particularly observed as *the real division of the orders of moldings when they all lie on* the chamfer-plane. The Decorated hollows are usually of larger size than the Early English; and there is this general difference in their use, that *in the Decorated they divide groups, in the Early English individual members.*

The exquisite skill, taste, and patient labour invariably evinced in the working of Early English moldings, are truly admirable. The ingenuity that was never at a loss in any difficulty of finish or constructive irregularity, and the minuteness with which even the most concealed and darkened parts were executed, are circumstances of much interest, if contrasted with the hasty and economical practice of the present day. The deepest hollows are all as cleanly and perfectly cut as the most prominent and conspicuous details; and in the village church as much so as in the most glorious cathedral. An Early English doorway is often a wonderful piece of art, however little it may attract the attention of ordinary observers. It is most pleasing to notice the long trails of dog-tooth lurking in the dark furrow of a label or chancelled recess; to see the end of some inconvenient member got rid of by throwing a flower across the point where it suddenly stops or dies into the wall; to admire the efflorescent boss and the foliaged capital intruding their luxuriance upon the moldings and hollows, as if they had overgrown their original and proper limits. How beautifully, too, the knots of pierced and hanging leaves extend like some petrified garland or bower of filigree-work round the arch, dividing the plainer moldings into groups, and almost imparting life and vegetation to the very stones! There are abundance of doorways of this style which exhibit the most delightful varieties in their forms and groupings; always, yet never, the same. Some examples occur at Bolton and Furness Abbeys, whose arch-moldings extend five or six feet in width. The west fronts of several of our cathedrals have Early English doorways of amazing magnificence. The entrance doorway of the Chapter House at Lichfield is a very fine example of the molding of this style. But almost every cathedral and every ruined abbey will supply good specimens, so that it would be useless to multiply illustrations. Plate XVIII. fig. 3, is a doorway in the cloisters at Peterborough; fig. 2, a doorway immediately opposite, in the south aisle of the nave, both on a scale of half an inch to one foot. Fig. 5 is a ruined doorway at Rivaulx Abbey. Fig. 6 is from the east window of Castle Rising Church; * fig. 7, from Beaulieu Abbey,† the southern triplet of the Refectory; fig. 8, an arch-mold from the choir of Ripon Minster; fig. 9 is borrowed from Brandon's Analysis of Gothic Architecture.

These latter examples (6, 7, 10) show the method of inserting the tooth ornament in, or rather across, hollows. Many of the more elaborate groups of Early English moldings contain several successive trails of this decoration, often of different sizes, shape, and planes of projection. In the very beautiful west doorway at Binham Priory, Norfolk, a curious variety of the dog-tooth is set in hollows of such depth, that the eye cannot fathom the point of attachment.

* This and fig. 10 from the same, are taken from Mr. Bowman's illustrations of that church, PL. VIII.

† From Weale's Quarterly Papers, Vol. II. PL. II.

SECTION VI.

OF DECORATED MOLDINGS.

DURING THE REIGNS OF THE FIRST THREE EDWARDS, 1272-1377.

The student will bear in mind that the *details* of Decorated moldings are in great measure identical with those of the preceding style, with the addition of some new members, and several important modifications of grouping. And the latter will be found to produce an entirely different effect, though in description the distinction may appear very trifling. The eye must be familiarized to the profile and general appearance of moldings of different dates, so that, without dismembering, and, as it were, analysing the group, or examining the separate details, it may discern at a glance the style to which any example belongs. And this may be done with a considerable degree of certainty by practice and attention; though it can hardly be asserted that *all* the differences of style admit of being reduced to unvarying and infallible rules. Sometimes moldings are met with of much earlier or later date than we should have expected from other characteristic marks in the building; and there are not a few instances in which, without the aid of such marks, it would be impossible to say whether a molding is of the fourteenth or the fifteenth century. In fact, this science does not appear capable of more than general treatment; though there is quite enough of uniform system to enable us to apprehend the broad distinctive principles which obtained in the different periods.

Generally, then, much greater geometrical precision may be observed in drawing both the hollows and the projecting members than prevailed in the preceding style. Segments of circles, both concave and convex, were much used, and there was a softness of blending, a delicacy and gentleness of grouping, an avoidance of strong and violent contrasts of light and shade, which imparted a more pleasing, though much less striking, effect.

Early English arch-moldings have sometimes a monotonous effect, which is but imperfectly remedied by the free use of quaint, irregular, and fanciful members. The reason is, first, that frequently the numerous members do not vary materially in size, and secondly, that each stands between two deep hollows, so that the entire group looks like a mere alternation of dark and light, repeated with little change several times over. Now the composition of Decorated moldings is essentially different. For not only do the members vary in size, but also in kind; the deep hollows are principally confined to the inner angles, and there is no extravagant isolation of small and unimportant parts. The roll-and-fillet is formed with as little undercutting as possible, as in PL. XVII. figs. 2, 3, 9, 10: in fact, only just enough is hollowed away at the sides to develope the outline.

Decorated roll-and-fillet.

In the Geometric-Decorated age (that is, in the reign of the first two Edwards), the moldings of arches and jambs differ very slightly from those of pure Early English; so slightly, indeed, that they cannot alone be taken as decisive of this or that date. It was not until the Flowing-Decorated era (that is, during the reign of Edward III.), that these moldings took the characteristic turn which brought about the surrender of the roll-and-fillet, and its many varieties, for the ogees, bowtells, and wide shallow casements of the Perpendicular period.

Rich Decorated moldings are of rather rare occurrence. A great many of the finest buildings in this style scarcely afford as good examples of molding as small and humble churches of the Early English age. Very often plain chamfers are used in all the windows, doorways, and pier-arches; while minor parts, such as bases, capitals, sedilia, sepulchral recesses, and the like, have fine and elaborate details. It is in this kind of work that we must look for the best moldings in the Decorated style. In arches, doorways, and windows, the plain chamfer of two orders (PL. I. fig. 5) is perhaps most commonly found. Windows especially are often singularly meagre in their moldings, however rich their tracery may be. The monials stand near the outer surface of the wall, and separated from or recessed behind it only by a single order with a plain or hollow chamfer, as PL. VII. figs. 20 and 21. Frequently, indeed, the tracery of good Decorated windows stands quite flush with the wall, so that the jamb-moldings are, as it were, entirely omitted.* And again, the monials and tracery often consist of merely chamfered planes, without any edge-lines to relieve them; and so, PL. VII. fig. 20, the east window at Trumpington. Fig. 19, a window at Hingham, Norfolk, is one degree richer than this, two orders being introduced in the monial, though of equally plain character.

There appear to be three distinct kinds to which Decorated moldings may generally be referred; though there are many examples which it might be difficult to assign to any one of them. These are :—

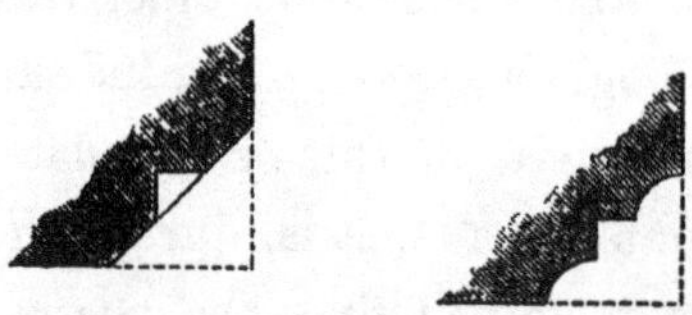

1. The plain or hollow chamfer of two or more orders, which, properly speaking, is only the step preparatory to molding, and stopping short of that ulterior process.

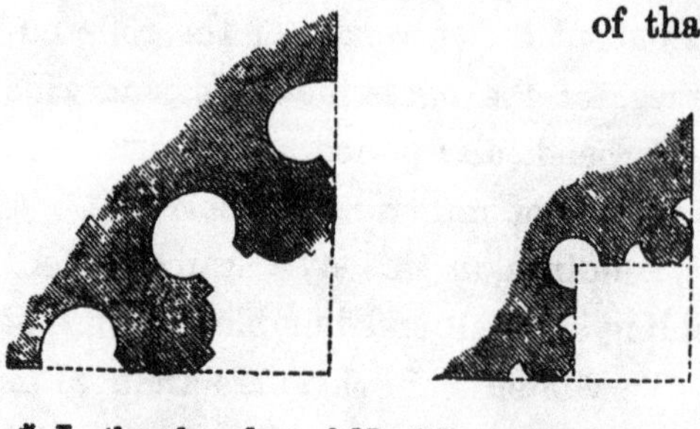

2. Roll - and - fillet moldings, with hollows between each member, nearly resembling, in principle and arrangement,

* In the churches of Norfolk and Suffolk this is the rule, and not the exception, from the scarcity of stone in those parts.

the Early English method, as in diagrams PL. V. fig. 12—a doorway at Attleborough, Norfolk, and PL. XVII. figs. 4, 6, 8.

3. A succession of double ogees, divided by hollows of three-quarters of a circle, as PL. VI. figs. 9, 11, 12, 14. PL. II. fig. 16, is similar in kind, and both of these are exceedingly common moldings in this style. It is not unusual to find these two varieties combined, as in PL. VII. fig. c—the belfry-arch at Deopham, Norfolk. And as they rarely occupy any other position than the chamfer-plane, it seems proper to regard them as virtually the plain chamfered edges of class 1, slightly relieved from their flat and naked form. Their distinctive peculiarity consists in the repetition of the same members in each order, though, as we have observed, other varieties of the chamfer are sometimes intermixed. Thus PL. VI. fig. 11, might be described in words thus:—"A double-ogee order between two hollow chamfer orders, divided by three-quarter hollows; all lying in the chamfer-plane of 45°; total width across, twenty-three inches."

The plain or hollow chamfer is extremely common in all jambs and archways (especially if they be continuous, or have no imposts or jamb-shafts), in the Early Decorated style. The inner angle which divides the orders (and which has been called the *re-entering angle*), is either left solid, or cut into a deep three-quarter hollow. Of this latter arrangement, which produces a very bold and good effect, it might be difficult to name a better example than the west doorway of St. Mary's, Ely. Here the chamfers are hollow, or quarter-circles. In such cases there are often trails of ball-flowers, quatrefoil pateræ, roses, or other ornamental leaf-work disposed at regular intervals, and repeated in rows in two or more of the chamfers. See PL. VI. fig. 2; PL. VII. fig. 10.

The second kind is generally, but not always, early in the style; and it is perhaps the most perfect and beautiful of all.

The members in this case usually fall in squares (that is, on the wall-planes and soffit-planes in succession), as in the west doorway at Trumpington Church, PL. VII. fig. 3. PL. XVII. fig. 3, is from the south porch of Bottisham Church, near Cambridge. Fig. 5 is from a doorway at Langham, Rutland, of the Geometric age. Fig. 8 is from the beautiful Decorated archway of the south porch, at Over, Cambridgeshire. Fig. 10 is a window jamb, from Grantham Church. Sometimes moldings of this class are combined with those of the third, as PL. V. fig. 11, the priest's door, at Hingham, Norfolk; PL. XVII. fig. 7, a doorway at Burfield, Suffolk; PL. XX. fig. 17, the chancel door at Willingham, near Cambridge; and PL. V. fig. 1, a monument at Boston. PL. VII. figs. 7, 8, 12, are all of this second kind.

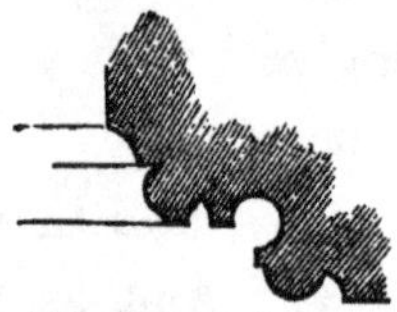

Window-jamb, Over.

There is, however, a perceptible difference in the shape of the Early English and the Decorated roll-and-fillet. In the later style the fillet is broader, not set square on the roll, and the neck is wider from the hollows between the single members, being less deeply undercut. The capricious and irregular forms of the earlier style are no longer found; the roll-and-triple-fillet, arranged upon rectangular lines, is generally one member of the group, and the gently bulging ogee curvature predominates throughout. In many instances the roll-and-fillet forms a member of very large size, as PL. XX. fig. 15, a monument in the choir of Bolton Abbey.

Decorated filleted rolls.

While moldings of the second kind are generally borne by jamb-shafts, as in the Early English style (though now engaged in, and not detached from, the wall), those of the first and third are almost always continuous,* except in pier-arches, where they constantly occur, in which case they are stopped by the capitals.

* In doorways the moldings borne by the jamb-shafts always lie on the rectangular planes, those which are continuous on the chamfer planes.—Analysis of Gothic Architecture, p. 68.

Thus, PL. VII. fig. 4, is a pier-arch at Trumpington; PL. VI. fig. 3, one at Hingham. Sometimes a series of four or five of these together, as PL. VI. fig. 12, gives a very deep and rich effect to a doorway. It is not uncommon to find one member of a double ogee considerably larger than the other, or those of one order of different size from the others. It must be particularly observed that in the third class of Decorated moldings the fillets on each side of the three-quarter hollows (*i. e.* the untouched portions of the rectangular nook) almost invariably stand at right angles with each other, the principle of which is shown at PL. V. fig. 3, the west doorway at Attleborough, Norfolk. Exceptions, such as PL. VII. fig. A, are seldom found in *ancient*, but very often in *modern* moldings. We may further observe on PL. V. fig. 3, that if the sides of the re-entering angle are equal, the chamfer-plane is the diagonal of a square, that is, it forms an angle of 45°. So, in PL. VII. fig. 2, the angle of the chamfer-plane is ascertained by measuring the two sides of the central nook. Sometimes the group appears to have been designed on the principle of a series of squares, as seen in PL. XVII. fig. 3.

Moldings are either *simple* or *compound*. A simple molding is a plain single form, complete in itself, as a bowtell or three-quarter round. A compound molding is either composed of two or more distinct parts, as a roll-and-fillet, a double ogee; or involves a profile of reflex or double curvature. This is properly the character of the ogee itself, which is formed by a segmental inward curve conjoined continuously with a similar outward curve. Of the same kind is a very important and universal Decorated form, which may be called the *compound ogee*, or the WAVE-MOLDING, from its gently undulating outline.* It is represented in PL. VII. figs. C, 9, 17, 18, 19, and elsewhere. It is composed of two ogee curvatures, forming a central bulge or

* Professor Willis calls this the *swelled chamfer*. Inigo Jones applied the term *wave* to the ogee. See Architectural Nomenclature, § 16.

entasis, sometimes projecting forward beyond the edges, but usually in the same plane with them. Scarcely any method of molding is so common in, or so characteristic of, this style, and especially of the *Flowing*, or later Decorated, to which era its use was principally confined. It frequently occurs with a hollow between, as PL. VII. fig. 17. The formation of this detail may be traced either to the ordinary edge roll being simply somewhat less undercut, or to the half of a triply filleted roll

Edge roll.

Triply filleted roll.

Half roll and fillet.

PL. IV. fig. 10, the other half being considered as undeveloped, or merged in the block; or to the insertion of a quarter-shaft into a rectangular nook, the edges at the points of junction being rounded instead of sharp and abrupt. The latter is not improbable on the analogy of the earlier and later (that is, the square and rounded) forms of the roll-and-fillet. Indeed, the form shown in the accompanying outline is sometimes found. It occurs in the sedilia at Elsworth Church, near Cambridge, and is represented in the "Guide to the Neighbourhood of Oxford," p. 333, from Garsington Church; and in PL. XXIV. of Potter's "Buildwas Abbey" (Early English). There are several modifications of it: the edges are either sharp, as PL. VII. fig. 17, or there is a small width of the chamfer-plane left uncut on each side,

The wave-molding.

Varieties of wave-molding.

as PL. V. fig. 11; PL. XX. fig. 1, a doorway from Landbeach Church, Cambridgeshire. In this case, the concaves are sometimes slightly undercut. The former is most common in Decorated, the latter in Perpendicular. It is so much more common in Decorated work, that its occurrence may, in default of other proofs, be taken as a presumptive evidence of the style. It is also wider and shallower in early than in late work; that is, the side hollows are less deep, and the central entasis less bulging.* Sometimes, indeed, the wavy line is so faint as to be scarcely different from the plain chamfer, as PL. VII. fig. A. And sometimes we find nothing more than a flat surface sunk between two raised edges. See PL. VII. fig. B, and the lowest order of fig. 8. This may be termed the *sunken chamfer*. It is not of very common occurrence; a very good specimen is engraved in the "Oxford Guide," p. 281, from Headington Church.

Another variety is shown in PL. VII. figs. 13, 16, 23, and PL. XX. fig. 2, a window-jamb from Quy Church, near Cambridge. This appears to have arisen from cutting down to an angle, instead of scooping out in an ogee curve, one end of the member. It is generally a mark of Transition to Perpendicular.

A rare form is exhibited in PL. V. fig. 16. It may be called a double wave-molding. By cutting the central hollow down to an angle (as shown in the shaded part), a double ogee would be the result. This molding occurs in the Decorated belfry-arch at Stretham, Isle of Ely, and in the east window of the south aisle at Bottisham, Cambridgeshire, PL. XIX. fig. 3.

A plain bowtell, or a roll-and-fillet, between two wave-moldings, is found in Decorated work. PL. XVII. fig. 2, is from the north porch of Bottisham Church, Cambridgeshire; fig. 1, from the outer archway of the south porch (fig. 3 being the inner) of the same church. In fig. 2, the rolls-and-fillets fall within, or short of, the rectangular plane, because they would otherwise have been too large.

* The formation is shown in PL. XIX. figs. 1 and 2. It will be seen that the early form involves the equilateral, the later the obtuse triangle. It is clear from PL. XIX. fig. 5. that this form was not unknown in Early English architecture. It also occurs, in the form approximating to the outline diagram in p. 50, in an archway at Croxden Abbey, circa 1240.

The ogee molding is a form so extensively used, and so difficult to explain fully in its origin and varied relations, that it is almost impossible to do more than point out its general and leading characteristics. In respect of its origin, the ogee curve is so prevalent in the Classic styles, that it might easily be supposed it was thence imported into the Gothic, were there not abundant opportunities of self-development presented by the varieties of the roll-and-fillet. It is believed that the ogee scarcely, if ever, occurs in Norman architecture, in England at least, whatever may be the case in the Romanesque edifices in other countries. Its occasional appearance in the Early English style, has been already mentioned, where, however, it is very sparingly used. It should be especially noted that whenever the ogee occurs in Decorated

moldings, it always suggests to the mind the idea of one side of a roll-and-fillet; the convex portion being much larger than the concave. In its most ordinary position in a window-jamb, it actually corresponds to a perfect roll-and-fillet in the monial, as PL. VII. figs. 9, 10, 11; and here it must, of course, be regarded literally as half of that member. Since, however, the

quirked ogee (see PL. XVI. fig. 2), so common in Classic edifices, is identical in form with this part of a monial (fig. 3), it seems extremely difficult to decide how far the form was introduced from this or that suggestion. But in this latter case, the earliest forms would be found of Classic character with the large concave portion, whereas we can actually trace its gradual formation from the roll-and-fillet, having at first the roll the predominant portion, and the hollow gradually gaining in importance in later work; so that it would not perhaps be saying too much to vindicate for Gothic architecture the self-development of the ogee, rather than refer it to an imitation of uncongenial Classic details.

The following, therefore, are the principal forms found in Decorated moldings:—

1. The roll-and-fillet.
2. Roll-and-triple-fillet.
3. Ogee.
4. Double ogee, or double ressant.
5. Scroll-molding, or ressant lorymer.
6. Wave-molding, or swelled chamfer.
7. Plain or hollow chamfer.
8. Sunken chamfer PL. VII. fig. B.

It is difficult to give a name to the form shown in PL. VII. fig. 16, and perhaps it is not of sufficiently frequent occurrence to render a particular term desirable.

Other minor varieties might be added of forms which are principally found in Decorated work. Sometimes a semicircle sunk in the chamfer-plane is found, as PL. VI. fig. 6, a doorway at Deopham, Norfolk; PL. VII. fig. 14, a fragment from Rivaulx Abbey; and PL. VI. fig. 13, a very fine archway at Hardingham, Norfolk; and PL. V. fig. 14, a window at Hingham. So also PL. V. fig. 2. This detail is the most usual in Transition to Perpendicular, *circa* 1360–80.

The bowtell, or three-quarter round, is used, but rather sparingly, in Decorated work; it was extremely common in Perpendicular. PL. VII. fig. 18, is a doorway of Transition date, at Swanton Morley, Norfolk, in which the bowtell occupying the centre forms an engaged shaft. When this is the case, the fillet is seldom wanting, except in very advanced work. But the plain roll appears in PL. V. figs. 1, 3, 5, all of which are late in the style.* Sometimes the bowtell is seen in juxtaposition with the sunken semicircle, as in PL. V. figs. 1, 4, 5.

In PL. VII. fig. 6, a window at Fen Stanton, a small tongue-

* All the examples in PL. V. are *late* Decorated. The occurrence of the small three-quarter round, as in figs. 1, 3, 4, 5, is a sure indication of approach to Perpendicular.

shaped member projects from the inner side of the principal roll-and-fillet. This should be noticed as a very characteristic detail of Decorated moldings of the second class, to which this example belongs. See also PL. XVII. fig 5. A combination extremely common in labels and capitals is shown in PL. XVI. fig. 48. This occurs also in jambs and arches, as PL. II. fig. 14.

PL. V. fig. 9, and PL. VI. figs. 14, 15, show the method of principal and secondary monials. The moldings are of course coincident in every part of the tracery and monials, and in the corresponding parts or planes of the jamb; so that, for shortness' sake, architects generally draw double monials, as in these examples, merged into one another. Thus the outer edge represents the actual profile of the jamb, which, as being identical in detail, may of course be also taken to represent one side of the monials. In drawing the section of a window-jamb, the monial-members may be represented by lines across, parallel with the wall-plane. PL. V. fig. 9, is the inner jamb of the east window at Heckington; PL. VI. fig. 14, the same part of a window in the chancel at Boston; PL. VI. fig. 15, is from Stoke Golding, Leicestershire.

When a window has primary and secondary monials, it is obvious that they carry distinct planes or orders of moldings. Yet these orders are not always of the same nature as those we have before described as such, namely, the group of members constituting the separate sub-arches; for the face of the smaller monial often falls within or behind that of the larger only by a single retiring step, or member of a group. Thus, in PL. VI. fig. 14, both the monials combined carry (properly speaking) the same order, but different members of it.

The plane in which the outer moldings of the jamb lie is seldom coincident, as in the last example, with that on which the monial members are arranged, for this would in most cases give too great thickness to the monials themselves, the slope or inclination of which must of course be the same on both sides of each aperture or light. The difference of inclination is sometimes very slight, but this point must be carefully attended to in copying moldings. See PL. VIII. fig. 5; PL. XX. fig. 8.

In Decorated windows, the face of the monials is generally a flat edge or fillet; but in some early examples, a roll-molding is carried all round, and is furnished with small bases resting on the cill. This roll-tracery is very common in Perpendicular windows; and sometimes, as at the west end of King's College Chapel, it has small stilted bases in the jamb.

Many Decorated windows have shafts in the jambs and monials both internally and externally. This produces a very fine effect, especially when the primary monials carry a triple, the secondary a single shaft. In these cases the moldings of the tracery follow the common law of pier-arches and shafted doorways, that is, they are different in section above the capitals. Ordinary windows, on the other hand, follow the principle of continuous archways.

The interior arch, or *rear-rib*, of Early English and Geometric windows is generally borne by a shaft,* except in very plain and inexpensive buildings. Shafts, in fact, form a very essential part in the composition of the more elaborate windows in these styles. The aisles and clerestory in the nave of St. Alban's Abbey, and the south choir-aisle of St. Mary's Church, Stafford, afford most beautiful instances of shafted window-jambs.

The labels or hood-moldings of the date of Edward I. and II. are often undercut by a three-quarter circle, sunk in the surface of the wall, as in PL. VI. figs. 1 and 10, doorways at Little Ellingham, Norfolk; fig. 8, the north doorway at Hingham; and fig. 13, at Hardingham. This latter example is unusually bold and deep. It measures three feet across from the

* Called anciently, the *rear-shaft*. Willis's Architectural Nomenclature, p. 57.

outer face of the label to the soffit, and the effect is remarkably fine. Fig. 5 is the interior of a window-jamb at Sleaford. Fig. 7 from a monument at Boston, the soffit at A. Fig. 4 is the molding of the pier-arches in the same church, of unusual and decidedly early character, though of rather late Decorated date.

PL. V. fig. 2 is a doorway at Great Ellingham. It closely resembles PL. VI. fig. 6. Fig. 4 is the inner doorway of the south porch at Boston. There is a close resemblance in the composition of this and of fig. 1, a monument in the same church, betraying the hand of the same artist. This resemblance should always be attended to, not only in the same church, but in the neighbouring edifices, because a strong presumption of coeval date is thence to be derived. And monuments especially were so often inserted subsequently, that it is very important to compare their moldings with other parts of the same church. The character of these two examples is rather late; and they are wiry and poor in their effect, from being cut away too deeply and widely from the block surface.

PL. V. fig. 5 is from a fine Decorated tomb at Ewerby Church, Lincolnshire; a noble structure, which almost rivals its immediate neighbour, the celebrated St. Andrew's, Heckington. This molding is a good and effective composition. It is shown in perspective, to illustrate the difference in appearance which exists between the same molding exhibited in section and in elevation. The roll-and-triple-fillet produces a fine effect in moldings of this style. Its edge-lines are sharp and delicate, and the profile beautifully relieved by the deep side-hollows with which it is necessarily connected.

PL. V. fig. 7 is the interior of a window-jamb at Bennington, Lincolnshire, and fig. 10 the exterior of the same. Fig. 8 is the interior of a window-jamb at Heckington. Fig. 13 is one side of the belfry-arch at West Keal, Lincolnshire.*

PL. VII. fig. 8 is the outer archway of the west entrance to

* This example is badly copied, and must not be depended upon.

the precinct, Peterborough; an effective Decorated group. Fig. 9 is a very common plan of a Decorated window. It is taken from Yaxley, Hunts. Fig. 10 is from Clipsham, Rutland—a window which is elegantly enriched by a trail of ball-flowers in the hollow chamfer of the outer order. Fig. 12 is a Decorated window from the chancel at Over; fig. 11, from Horbling, Lincolnshire. This also is a very common form in Decorated windows. Fig. 13 is from the outer porch doorway at North-borough. Fig. 15, a groin-rib from Rivaulx Abbey; fig. 16, a doorway from West Keal; fig. 21 is a window from the fine Decorated chancel at Keddington, or Ketton, Suffolk. Fig. 22, the molding at the angle of a piscina, Thurlby, Lincolnshire. Fig. 23, the south doorway at Langtoft, near Market Deeping.

PL. XX. fig. 4 is an archway in the cloisters at Peterborough, with double jamb-shafts.

SECTION VII.

OF PERPENDICULAR MOLDINGS.

FROM THE ACCESSION OF RICHARD II. TO DEATH OF HENRY VIII.*

A.D. 1377 TO 1546.

In the moldings of this style a debasing influence will at once be perceived in the comparatively meagre *save-trouble* method of working them. Large and coarse members, with little of minute and delicate detail, wide and shallow hollows, occupying spaces which, in early work, would have been filled with groups of separate moldings; hard wiry edges in place of rounded and softened forms, and general shallowness of

* This might fairly be divided by the student into Perpendicular and Tudor, commencing the latter with the reign of Henry VII., 1485.

cutting, are all conspicuous characteristics. Add to these, that their general arrangement on the chamfer-plane, which is a marked feature of the Perpendicular period, gives a flatness which is unpleasing to the eye in comparison with the rectangularly recessed grouping of the two preceding styles. At the same time, there is such a mass of really high art in the work of this period, that the student must be careful not to slur it over, in indulging any predilection he may have formed for earlier work. The moldings of this style frequently die into a basement composed of the simple uncut chamfer-plane, in which case the outer edges of each molding, of course, coincide with it, since it is only by cutting channels that the moldings are developed from it. Three peculiarities are so common in Perpendicular moldings, that their absence almost forms the exception to general usage. These are:—

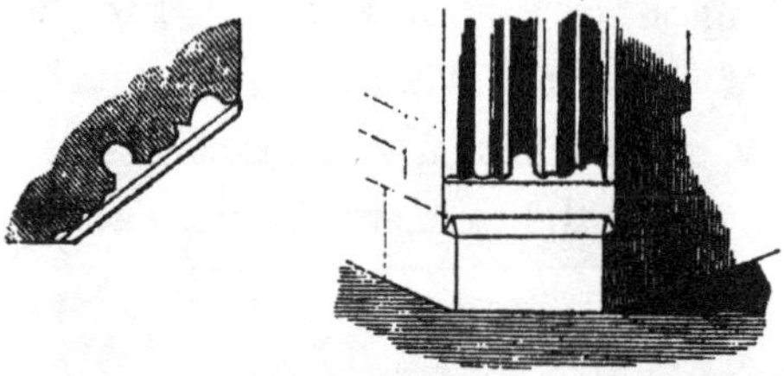

Fireplace, Vicar's Close, Wells.

1. A wide shallow casement, or hollow, usually occupying the centre of the group, and equal to about one-third of the width;

2. The constant use of bowtells, or beads, of three-quarters of a circle, resembling small shafts, and often used as such;

3. The frequency of the double ogee, and some varieties of it peculiar to the period.

The casement alluded to may undoubtedly be regarded as an elongation or extension of the Decorated three-quarter hollow, by which width is gained at the sacrifice of depth. Accordingly, it is generally a mark of early Perpendicular work when the casement is deep and narrow, of late when wide and shallow, and of debased when it is, as it were, so stretched as to become almost or quite a flat surface, sunken but little below the chamfer-plane, or external line of the group. The latter result may be observed in the windows of St. Botolph's Church, and in those of the older portions of St. John's College, Cambridge.

Of many forms which the casement assumes, the most frequent are those represented in PL. IX. figs. 11, 16, and PL. VIII. figs. 4, 10, 13. It is very common to find one or both ends of the hollow returned in a kind of quasi-bowtell, as seen in PL. VIII. figs. 2 and 15, and PL. XX. fig. 3, a window in the chancel of Grantham Church. Frequently, however, perhaps generally, the ends are sharp and angular, as PL. IX. fig. 14, PL. XX. fig. 14, the arch-mold of the nave of Lancaster Church, or PL. VIII. fig. 3. The three-quarter hollow also occurs in this style, and sometimes, as in PL. IX. fig. 2, in the same group with the great casement or central hollow.

The bowtell will be observed in some form or other in almost every example given in PL. VIII. and IX.; and if the student compares the three plates of Decorated moldings, he will perceive the importance of assigning this feature as a *peculiarity* of the Perpendicular. In PL. XX. fig. 6, from Rivaulx Abbey, a small double bowtell forms the central member. Fig. 10, the western doorway at Newton Church, near Cambridge; figs. 11 and 12, both from Bolton Abbey; fig. 13, from a small doorway in the choir of Grantham Church; and fig. 5, a doorway in Ripon Minster,—all contain examples of the cylindrical bowtell. It is often formed from a plane by sinking a channel on each side, as in PL. VIII. figs. 1, 3, 6. Occasionally it stands like an excrescence on the surface of a plane, as fig. 5; but this is a departure from the usual practice, as well as from the true principle of moldings.

The double ogee is much more common in Perpendicular than in Decorated moldings. There is some difference, too, in the form which it assumes in the later style. For whereas the Decorated ogee, as before stated, always represents the profile of the half of a roll-and-fillet, the Perpendicular appears rather to be composed of a semicircular hollow continued in a bowtell, forming a section more like the letter S—see PL. XVI. figs. 4 and 5. However, the earlier form, fig. 5, is extremely common in Perpendicular moldings, and especially in the double ogee. Other varieties, peculiar to the style, are the double ogee with a bowtell in the centre, PL. IX. fig. B; an ogee combined with a quarter-circle,* fig. C; an ogee with a small bead or fillet at the base, as PL. VIII. figs. 7, 9; an ogee with a bowtell forming one side of the great casement, PL. IX. figs. 1, 8, 10, 16, 17; and the combination exhibited in fig. 15, where the depth of the hollow is generally conclusive. All these may be considered as distinctive criteria of the style.

Perpendicular members.

The form represented in outline in the preceding woodcut is found in all the styles. It occurs in Early English work, with the roll or bowtell plain and not filleted, in a doorway at Fountains Abbey. The shape, however, of the ogee curve and the breadth of the fillet will be found to follow the rules laid down.

The double ogee is sometimes of large and clumsy size in Perpendicular arch-moldings. In Decorated, it is usually rather small, and is principally confined to the outer members of doorways and windows. A roll-and-fillet between two ogees is properly a late Decorated combination, as in PL. II. fig. 14; PL. VII. fig. 3. In PL. VIII. fig. 16, the inner doorway of the south porch at Great Shelford, near Cambridge, it is of the Transition period, that is, before 1400.

The form of the roll-and-fillet, prevalent in this style, in which, however, it was not extensively used,† is that between PL. IV. figs. 10 and 11. The debased form of the bowtell mold,

* This is one of the commonest and most decisive combinations in Perpendicular moldings, as PL. XX. figs. 10 and 14; PL. IX. fig. 3.

† The absence of the roll-and-fillet, except in a very corrupted form, is, in fact, one of the most remarkable features in the moldings of the late Gothic. When it does occur, it usually springs from the capital of a small bowtell.

PL. VIII. fig. 21, is also peculiar to the style; it is much used in basement moldings and capitals. Sometimes we find the roll-and-triple-fillet in a debased form, as in PL. IX. fig. 13, the belfry-arch at Haslingfield, Cambridgeshire. Two other corrupted varieties are exhibited in fig. 16. In the annexed diagrams the upper figure represents the Early English; the other two, varieties of the Perpendicular roll-and-fillet.

A half roll-and-fillet frequently occurs, as in PL. XX, fig. 7, a window-jamb from the south aisle of the nave at Ripon Cathedral; fig. 9, a doorway from Bolton Abbey. The pointed bowtell is very rare in this style; it is shown in fig. 3, and it occurs in the aisle windows at the west end of St. John's Church, Stamford.

Window-moldings are usually extremely meagre, though the tracery is generally set deeper in the wall than in the preceding style, and, consequently, a larger space is available for the purpose. But the great casement, or hollow, encroaches so much upon the group that little room is left for more than a double ogee on the outside of it, and the monial-members on the inside —by which term those moldings of the jamb are meant which coincide with the monials. PL. VIII. fig. 12, represents the almost universal plan of Perpendicular windows. Sometimes, however, especially in earlier examples, we find the double ogee externally, comprising the first order, and the monial-members occupying the next, without any casement in the angle. PL. IX. figs. 12 and 18, are taken from different churches, and illustrate the remarkable uniformity which prevailed in the use of moldings.

Having pointed out these facts (which deserved to be registered as essential and characteristic differences), little remains to be said on this part of the subject. Rich and good Perpendicular moldings are not very common, most examples consisting but of three or four very ordinary members, which offer nothing either novel or interesting to the view; while in the two preceding styles there is ever something singular, or beautiful, or ingenious, in the treatment of the moldings, to arrest our attention and add to our store of knowledge. But Perpendicular work is by no means to be despised, for many points may be found, such as the jamb-shafts in deeply recessed doorways, which form groups of considerable delicacy.

PL. VIII. fig. 1, is from the west doorway at Uffington, near Stamford; early in the style. Fig. 2, is the same, from the isolated tower at Dereham, Norfolk. Fig. 3 the same, from Saham Toney; fig. 4 from Fishtoft, Lincolnshire. Fig. 5 is from the east window at Leverton, in the same county; fig. 6 from Partney; fig. 7 from Louth, both doorways; fig. 8 from Stewton, a window-jamb; fig. 9 from an oriel window in Lincoln; fig. 12 from the south Choir Chapel, Lincoln Cathedral; fig. 10 the east window at Chesterton, near Cambridge; fig. 13 an arch in St. Sepulchre's Church; fig. 14 from a niche at Great Gransden, near St. Neots; fig. 15 the east window at Stapleford, near Cambridge; fig. 16 from Great Shelford; fig. 17 a pier-arch from Holy Trinity, Colchester; fig. 18 the same from Long Melford, Suffolk; fig. 19 a doorway at St. Martin's, Stamford; fig. 20 the pier-arches of the same church; fig. 21 from Louth.

PL. IX. fig. 1, is from the east window of St. Martin's, Stamford; fig. 2 the west doorway of the same; fig. 3 the same from St. John's Church, Stamford; fig. 4 from the Bede House in that town; fig. 5 is from a pier-arch in the noble church of All Saints; fig. 6 the west doorway, and fig. 7 a window, from Histon, near Cambridge; fig. 8 is from the chancel door at Skirlaugh, Yorkshire;* fig. 9 the north doorway at Harlton, near Cambridge; fig. 10 the south doorway,

* The two moldings, figs. 8 and 10, are borrowed from the "Churches of Yorkshire," and figs. 11 and 16, from Messrs. Brandon's excellent work, the "Analysis of Gothic Architecture."

Skirlaugh; fig. 11 from Basingstoke, Hampshire; fig. 12 a window of common form; fig. 13 the belfry-arch at Haslingfield; fig. 14 the south doorway at Grantchester; fig. 15 a molding of constant occurrence; fig. 16 from St. Albans; fig. 17 a doorway, and fig. 18 a window, from Ryhall, Rutland. The former has large sculptured pateræ in the central casement.

It will be observed that the distinction of the *orders* is often completely lost in this style, while it is seldom undefinable in Decorated moldings. It also appears from the examples given, that in many cases the chamfer-plane is either more or less than an angle of 45°; and that occasionally, as PL. VIII. fig. 11, two parallel planes are taken for the basis of the arrangement.

The casement is sometimes so extravagantly hollowed as to give the appearance, and probably the actual effect, of weakening the jamb. This is a great fault, and always produces a very unsatisfactory result to the eye, which desiderates the idea of perfect and substantial support.* An instance may be noticed in the west window of Grantchester Church.

One principle of composition may sometimes be traced in moldings, especially in late ones. This is the custom of ending with a repetition of the same members which commenced the group, the centre being occupied by a different one. This may be illustrated by PL. IX. figs. 3, 6, 8, or by the annexed cut.

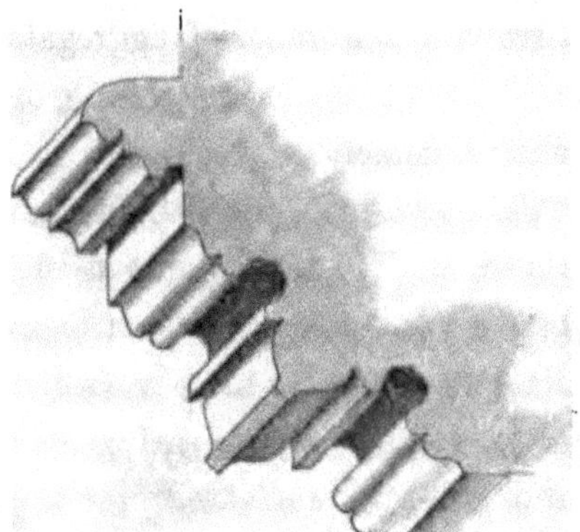

West doorway, Overstrand, Norfolk.

Students of the present subject will find a very valuable series of illustrations of base, capital, and arch-molds of the three styles in pp. 76, 77, of

* Willis's Architecture of the Middle Ages, p. 15.

Professor Willis's Architectural History of Winchester Cathedral, published by the Archæological Institute, and in many other accounts of cathedrals by the same author.

SECTION VIII.

OF THE PLANS OF GOTHIC COLUMNS.*

THIS subject falls properly under the head of Moldings, since the forms of piers or columns more or less partake of the details of the arch-moldings. But it is one of such extensive scope that only a few general rules can here be given for distinguishing the styles. And of these the bases and capitals will generally afford the surest indications.

A few sections have been given for the purpose in PL. III.

The general plan of the columns which support the nave or other principal arches, is either square, circular, octagonal, diamond-shaped, or parallelogramic; and these forms are either simple or complex.

Simple, when composed of one plain member, that is, not involving a number of aggregate parts;

Complex, when consisting of a core surrounded by smaller shafts, detached or engaged.

The earliest form of column is the circular, as is proved by those in the ancient chapel in the White Tower, London (probably the earliest piece of Norman architecture in England); also at Waltham Abbey (which, whether Harold's Church or not, is undoubtedly early) most of the columns are circular; and at Norwich Cathedral, St. Sepulchre's Church, Cambridge, and many other places, examples may be found. Polygonal

* The medieval terms for columns, capitals, and shafts, were respectively *pillars*, *chapiters*, and *verges*. The plinth, or footing of the columns, was the *patin*. See Professor Willis's Architectural Nomenclature, pp. 39–41.

Norman piers, of vast size and strength, support the eastern transept walls at Peterborough Cathedral. And these simple forms continued in common use throughout the Transitional, Early English, and Decorated periods in ordinary parochial churches, where they are sometimes disposed alternately, or in opposite rows. But a very common arrangement is that of the square plan, or forms derived from it; thus it was sometimes cut with angular recesses, like the arch and sub-arch, and these recesses were soon filled with small shafts. With circular columns the vaulting shafts were commonly stopped above the capitals by a corbel, but they were frequently brought down to the ground with the rectangular plan, where the flat face of the pier was continuous with that of the wall; and the member also carrying the sub-arch was often made into a semicircular form. Thus we obtain, though in a heavy and simple form, a regular clustered shaft, which, during the Early English period, was brought to a wonderful degree of lightness and elegance.

These complex Early English piers are often extremely beautiful; more so, perhaps, than those of any other style. They are so varied in arrangement that it would be impossible in this place to do more than notice their general characteristics, which consist principally in the number of smaller isolated shafts clinging to a central column, to which they are at intervals attached, in reality as well as in appearance, by molded bands or fillets. These shafts are generally of native marble,* or of some other kind of stone than the central pillar. The clustered capitals and bases are often worked out in one large piece.

A circular column, surrounded by four, six, or eight smaller

* It is a curious fact that the medieval English architects appear *never* to have used any foreign marbles, in construction at least. The Purbeck limestone, composed of comminuted freshwater shells (whence it is called *lumachella marble*), being part of the Wealden formation, and taking a fine polish, though liable to disintegrate, was much used in the thirteenth century, but much more sparingly afterwards, except for tombs and the beds of sepulchral brasses.

detached shafts, is a beautiful and common device. Examples are very common; the choir-aisles at Ely, the Lady Chapel of Fountains Abbey (PL. XIX. fig. 8), and many parts of Westminster Abbey, have this kind of compound pillar. In some cases the column is made up of several shafts, generally four, placed close together, without any central core, as in the round nave of the Temple Church. In this case there is always a midway band or bonding-stone, worked into annular fillets to the shafts. The shafts are not always separately applied, though usually so in the pure lancet style. PL. III. fig. 11, is an instance of attached shafts so deeply undercut that they have the appearance of complete isolation. It forms an exquisitely graceful feature in the Chapter House of Furness Abbey. The lower part of a similar one, rather later in date, still stands in the vestibule of St. Mary's Abbey, York; and there is a very good example at Exton, Rutland. PL. III. fig. 8, is from All Saints, Stamford; fig. 13 from Ruskington, Lincolnshire; and fig. 12 from St. Peter Gowt's, at Lincoln. Fig. 17 is from Skelton, near York; and this is a very common form of Early English and Decorated piers, with some varieties, as fig. 16 and in PL. V. figs. 15, 17. PL. XIX. fig. 5, is a beautiful example of the former style, from Stretton Church, Rutland. Fig. 6 is from Grantham Church. The annexed is from Ruskington Church, Lincolnshire, and is reduced from the section given in Mr. Bowman's illustrations of that church.

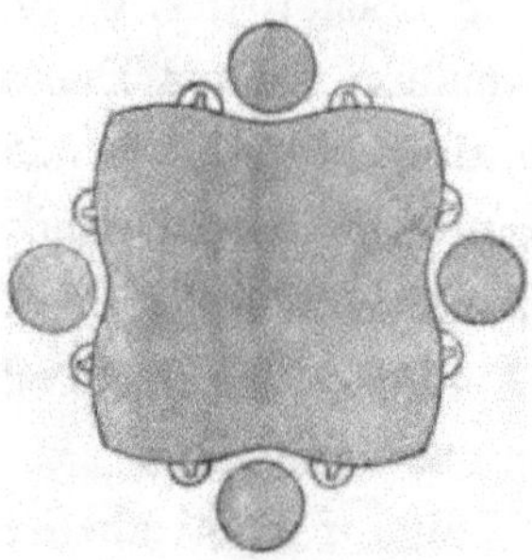

Ruskington.

Half of a roll-and-fillet set on each side of a square, the corners of which project, and are sometimes worked into smaller pointed beads, is of constant occurrence. The square being set to the cardinal points, the addition of the shafts changes the outline to the diamond form. The fillets running up the face of each shaft usually pass over or round the astragal, and die into the bell of the capital, as in PL. X. fig. 40.

Towards the Geometric era, that is, after 1240, the shafts (or *verges*, as they were anciently called) began to be generally engaged, or attached to the central mass.* This will be seen in the choir of the Temple Church, erected at the above period. The construction, therefore, is entirely different, the whole diametric section being worked out of one block, for the sake of greater strength. Decorated piers always have their shafts engaged, so that a clustered column is in reality formed by channelling the surfaces of the mass in lines and hollows of graceful lights and shadows. PL. III. figs. 14 and 16, are among the commonest forms; but the richness and extent of the great piers in cathedrals and abbeys it would require a volume to set forth. Fig. 14 is from Utterby, Lincolnshire, and is remarkable for the hollow faces, which are seldom found but in small shafts in Perpendicular work.

Perpendicular piers are generally of oblong or parallelogramic plan, the longitudinal direction extending from *north to south.* On the east and west sides half-shafts are attached, which bear the innermost order, or soffit-moldings, of the arch; the rest, including the great casement or hollow, being usually continuous, without the interruption of any impost. Very good examples exist at Great St. Mary's, Cambridge, where vaulting-shafts are also added on the northern and southern faces. PL. III. fig. 15, is from Attleborough, Norfolk, of late Decorated date. PL. III. fig. 18, from St. John's, Stamford,

Grantham.

* Shafts ceased to stand detached or banded into clusters, and became instead firmly compacted into a mass; the bands, no longer of any use, real or apparent, being suppressed.—Brandon's Analysis, p. 2.

a plain but good illustration of this almost universal method. PL. XIX. fig. 4, from Saffron Walden, Essex. The principle which led to this form was the desire to obtain width in the direction of the thickness of the wall, combined with the least possible bulk, and the greatest span between the columns. In this they followed the plan of window monials; in fact, in some late churches, as at Swavesey, near Cambridge, they become nothing more nor less than exaggerated monials with shafts attached to carry the sub-arch.

Swavesey.

Another form, however, occurs not unfrequently in Perpendicular columns, which is shown in PL. III. figs. 19 and 20, the first from St. Martin's, the second from St. Mary's, Stamford. In these the ground-plan is a square, and each face (as in fig. 19), or each angle (as fig. 20), if set diamond-wise, carries an engaged shaft. In the first case, the angles are chamfered away; in the second, a hollow is sunk in the face between the shafts. This is usually of later date than the parallelogramic plan. Still, examples are not wanting of early Perpendicular character, as in Long Ashton Church, Somersetshire,* built about, or rather before, 1400. The nave columns in this church consist of a square, with a three-quarter circular shaft engaged in each face, the angles being cut away into the wave-molding, which runs continuously round the arches. PL. XIX. fig. 7, represents a column of good Decorated date in the crypt at Grantham, in which the same principle of formation is exhibited.

Wood Ditton Church.

The parallelogramic plan is sometimes found in Decorated columns, but

* Engraved in Bowman's Specimens of Ecclesiastical Architecture, PL. IV.

not until the close of the style. The marginal woodcut represents such a column from Wood Ditton Church, near Newmarket. An instance is given in "The Oxford Architectural Guide," p. 139, from Ensham Church, c. 1400.

SECTION IX.

OF CAPITALS.

THE moldings of capitals and bases form not the least interesting, extensive, and important part of the study. And they have the peculiar advantage of being more definitely marked, in the various periods of architecture, than any other kind of moldings. It is by no means impossible, even for an experienced eye, to mistake the details of a Decorated for those of a Perpendicular archway; but no one moderately acquainted with the subject could hesitate in pronouncing the style of a capital or base, provided it possessed any character at all.

To go very rapidly through the history of a column, we may suppose that an upright post planted in the earth was found to sink, or decline from the perpendicular, by a great superincumbent pressure. This failure suggested the necessity of a plinth, or broad footing of masonry, on which it might stand firm, erect, and immovable. This arrangement we may often observe in the construction of wooden sheds or rustic homesteads of rude timber-work. Again, a great square stone would naturally be placed upon the top of the pillar or post, as the bed or cushion to receive the superstructure, whether arch or entablature. It was from such an origin that the highly elaborated Gothic base and capital arose.

Examples fully as rude as this do actually exist in English

ecclesiastical architecture, so that we have positive fact to guide us instead of mere theory. The Ante-Norman belfry-arches at Barnack and St. Mary Bishophill Junior, York, with a great many others of probably much later date, have square pillars on each side, resting upon and surmounted by rude and clumsy blocks of stone.

In the Norman period, when the shaft was round, the highest and lowest members only, respectively called the *abacus* and the *plinth* (anciently the *patin*) were square, the parts immediately below the one and above the other being rounded off to suit the shape of the shaft. How this was

Cushion Capital.

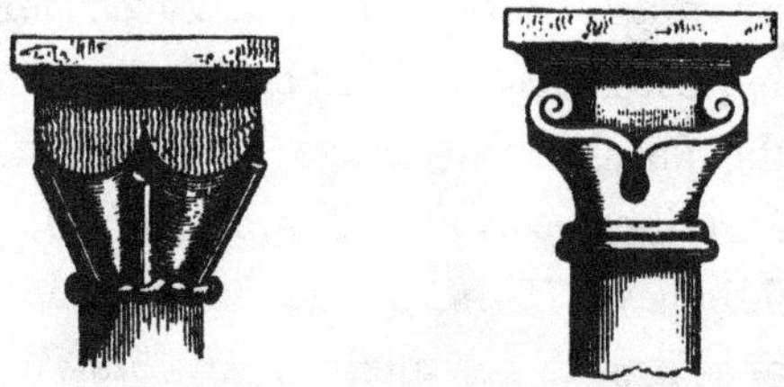

Transition Norman Capitals, Bolton Abbey.

done in Norman capitals is shown in PL. X. fig. 2, and it is seen in the ordinary form of what has been called the *cushion capital.* The lingering reluctance to get rid of the square plinth, in the tongue-shaped leaves or other grotesques which are often seen to issue from the circular moldings of Transition-Norman bases, and extend to the otherwise vacant and superfluous angles of the plinth, is worthy of observation. It was felt that these angles were not necessary; but the mediæval builders preferred to decorate what as yet they did not wish to cut away. Even in the advanced Early English columns in Westminster Abbey, instances of floriated bases may be observed.

But the simple square was sure to undergo some changes, and this took place first in capitals. In the more elaborate Classic styles, the sides were cut out, or curved inwards—a feature sometimes seen in Perpendicular octagonal capitals;

but this method of relieving and lightening the massive impost does not seem to have occurred to the Romanesque builders. They either cut off or cut out the corners, as soon as the pier-arch, by becoming recessed or involving a sub-arch (PL. I. fig. 4), left a portion of the bearing surface unemployed and superfluous. That is, rectangular nooks were cut in the angles of the square abacus, corresponding to the graduation of the sub-arch, as in the accompanying cut, and examples may also be seen in Potter's Illustrations of Buildwas Abbey, pl. 6. From the former process came the octagonal form; and either by removing angles indefinitely, or, more probably, by adopting the shape of the shaft, we obtain the circular capital and base of the first and second Gothic periods. But capitals became octagonal before plinths; and similarly octagonal plinths were retained long after circular capitals had become universal.

Ely: South Transept.

Gothic capitals may be divided into two kinds, molded and floriated. The upper member, or abacus, is common to both, and is the relic of the rude impost which first surmounted the stone post, from which it was transferred, through the medium of the Classic to the Christian styles. This seems, in fact, to be the primary and essential, and, as it were, *practical* member, the others being only decorative adjuncts. The lowest member, called the *neck* or *astragal*, is also common to both kinds; but in floriated capitals foliage covers the intermediate space, which is otherwise occupied by the overhanging and undercut member called the *bell*, with its accompanying moldings. In the Transition-Norman and Early English, the foliage, as is well known, is arranged vertically; in the Decorated it twines horizontally, or rather transversely, round the capital. In Perpendicular, floriated capitals are rare; more frequently small leaves, or *pateræ*, are set like studs at intervals round the shaft above the neck, as in Great St. Mary's Church, Cambridge. But the vine and the strawberry leaf is sometimes seen, very differently worked, however, from the deep overhanging foliage of the earlier styles, being only a shallow kind of surface ornament.

The dog-tooth, the nail-head, the ball-flower, and other ornamental moldings, sometimes occur in capitals, and in later work the Tudor flower, or crestings of minute battlements (occasionally floriated), are also frequently found. Even angels' heads with spread wings are sometimes found, as in the belfry-arch of Great Shelford, near Cambridge, and in the choir of Wingfield Church, Suffolk. Occasionally (in Norman work commonly) some subject is grotesquely sculptured below the abacus. Of this there is a very curious example at West Keal, Lincolnshire.* Or a subject is intermixed with the foliage, as in some very interesting Early English capitals in the south transept and the north porch of Wells Cathedral.

But of floriated or sculptured work it is not at present our province to speak. It is enough to observe that the origin of foliage is probably Classical, since in the Romanesque we find the style of it, as used in capitals, very closely approaching the Corinthian acanthus, or the Ionic volute; for example, the Transitional Norman capitals at the east end of Canterbury Cathedral, and not unfrequently in parochial churches (as at Barnack), seem clearly to be Classical in general features, and almost so in their details. Others, however, will have it that the origin of the foliated capitals is rather from the East. There can be little doubt that the influence of both prevailed in the introduction of foliage into Gothic capitals, from whence it was subsequently transferred to other parts of buildings.

* On one of the capitals (which are Decorated) a fox is carrying off a goose, while a chained ape is laying hold of it behind. The Decorated capitals in Oakham Church exhibit the same design, among others. This kind of capital may be called *Pictorial*, as the author has suggested in the Manual of Gothic Architecture, p. 110.

The *use* of capitals, in pure Gothic architecture, to speak constructively, is to receive the clusters of arch-molds which are stopped by it at the summit of the column, and not continued down to the ground. For, when the arch-molds are not wholly identical with those of the jamb or column, they must either die away at the spring (in which case they are called *discontinuous*) or be abruptly stopped by a projecting impost. In many cases the moldings are partly continuous and partly stopped by the capitals; certain groups being borne by shafts,* while the intervening hollows are continued to the ground, forming at the same time deep lines of division between the groups of arch-molds above and the separate jamb-shafts below. This is particularly the case in Perpendicular piers and arches, as described in Section VII. Here the soffit or innermost moldings, are borne by a shaft, the outer being continuous; while in Early English doorways the soffit is generally continuous, the others carried by shafts, as in PL. II. figs. 18 and 19. Again, in Norman and Early English, the shafts stand isolated; in the latter so far that the hand, or even the arm, may be passed round them. In Decorated, they are engaged, fewer in number, less prominent, less important in the apparent work of support. And in Perpendicular they become entirely subordinate, and merely decorative, as may be observed in the porches and doorways of King's College Chapel. Hence, by an ulterior debasement, mere bowtells, as we before remarked, are furnished with quasi-capitals and bases. In some cases a member of the same projection and diameter as the bowtell is continued above this quasi-capital (if the term be allowable), but slightly varied in form and profile.

The moldings of pier-arches became entirely continuous only in very late work; and the reason is, that the idea of a capital

* By what is called *decorative, i.e.* apparent construction. The moldings would in reality remain in their places as well without as with the bearing shafts.—Willis's Architecture, Chap. II.

or impost is essential to that of an isolated column; while in the jambs of doorways and entrance arches, the shafts themselves, and therefore the impost, may be omitted or added at will, as a mere matter of decoration.

A good Gothic capital is a feature of remarkable beauty. Take for example, those of the piers in the nave of Trumpington Church, Cambridge, and Hingham, Norfolk, PL. XII. figs. 11 and 15, or the woodcuts on pages 76, 77. Small in projection, complex and graceful in their members, yet judiciously subordinate to both arch and pier, they seem to bind into one the bundles of shafts which form the column, while, by their reversed or horizontal outlines, they intercept and at the same time form a satisfactory termination to the vertical lines above and below.

Gothic capitals consist of three parts; the abacus, the bell, and the neck. And these parts are distinctly visible in block capitals, or those in which the members have not been worked out. Such may occasionally be met with in village churches.

PL. X. fig. 1, shows the two uppermost members in their rudest state. Fig. 3 is from Laceby, Lincolnshire; fig. 4 from Middle Rasen, and fig. 5 from Walesby, both in the same county. Here A is the abacus, B the bell, C the neck. It will be observed that Gothic capitals may generally be reduced to this outline, as fig. 16, from Great Abington, Cambridgeshire.

The most certain evidence of date is furnished by the moldings of the abacus. The earlier forms of the abacus had the

Coton. St. Sep. Cambridge. Cant. Cath. Crypt. Blatherwick, Northants. Byland. Heacham, Norfolk. Wadenhoe, Northants.

upper edge always left square, and the under edge rather plainly chamfered or cut into a flat ovolo; at first the fillet was large in proportion, and gave a heavy appearance, but the lower edge-mold gradually became more important, and was frequently cut into a hollow chamfer and sometimes quirked and finished also with a bead, as at Heacham, Norfolk. By this means a light abacus was obtained, which held its ground far into the Early English style, as may be seen at the Refectory, Rivaulx, &c.

But then they began to cut away the upper edge, the projection was made greater, and the under side was cut or hollowed out, so that it seems to overhang the bell just as the bell does the shaft, and with the same profile, consisting of the half of a roll-and-fillet. The Decorated abacus has the scroll-molding, with a cylindrical roll of rather less size below it. PL. X. figs. 38 and 39, represent these peculiarities, and an examination of the sections of capitals of both styles will show how rarely this distinctive mark is wanting. In Early English capitals the abacus is sometimes quite plain, as fig. 17, from Thurlby, and fig. 8, from Frieston, Lincolnshire. In the reign of Edward I. a peculiar molding occurs, something between the two, which may be called an undercut scroll-molding. This is seen in fig. 9, from Stickney, and fig. 12, from Lincoln Cathedral, and it may be considered a characteristic of transition from Early English to Decorated.

The moldings of the bell are generally kept within the limits shown in fig. 5, but in very minute work exceptions are sometimes found; for instance, at Temple Balsal, Warwickshire, the capitals* to the small shafts on the monials of some of the windows, have the bell projecting quite beyond the abacus. Where foliage is introduced it often projected a long way even in large capitals, and a molding seems to have been allowed the same license when the scale was small. Small capitals and bases appear frequently to have been turned in lathes, and this might account for treating a molding like foliage where the effect of foliage was desired. In Early English capitals the bell has sometimes a double set of moldings, which gives a very hand-

* Figured in Bowman and Crowther's Churches of the Middle Ages.

some effect. This is seen in PL. X. figs. 19, 28, from Tintern, fig. 22, from Furness, and fig. 24, from Bolton.

Capitals occur in their greatest perfection in shafts. The larger piers, of octagonal or circular form, are seldom so elaborate or so decidedly marked. In these the abacus is the only member which affords any sure indication of date.

The distinguishing feature of Decorated capitals has been stated to be the scroll-molding of the abacus, and in perhaps

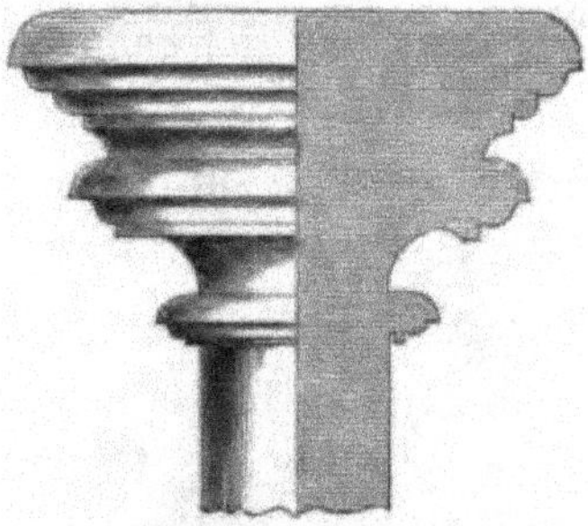

Decorated Capital, Grantham.

ninety-nine out of every hundred examples the rule holds good. Yet some capitals presenting the same feature are said to be of Early English date. It is believed that the Early English abacus scarcely ever occurs in pure Decorated work.

The bell is seldom so prominent or so deeply undercut in this as in the preceding style. As a general rule, the projection (*i.e.* the relative diameter to that of the shaft) became gradually less, both in capitals and bases, as the styles advanced. The above cut furnishes an exception to the rule. Thus, in Perpendicular work, when the shafts became, as it were, mere parts of the entire groups of moldings, both these features became minute and subordinate. Decorated capitals preserve the happy medium between the clumsiness of constructive members, and the inutility of mere ornaments. In this their remarkable beauty really consists, in that they occupy the truest and most consistent position as architectural parts of the whole. With respect to their details, the moldings of the bell present the principal varieties; but these are generally some modification or

corruption of the roll-and-fillet. Very often the under part of the bell is composed of an entire roll-and-fillet, as in PL. XII. figs. 3, 8, and PL. XI. figs. 12, 20. It is still more frequently formed by the compound member shown in the cut, and in PL. XI. fig. 4.

Out of forty-three examples of Decorated capitals given in PL. XI. and XII. ten of them have the bell thus formed, and others present some slight variety of it. It is seen in elevation in PL. XII. fig. 15, the beautiful capital of the nave-piers at Hingham.

Decorated capitals seldom have double moldings to the bell, at least much less frequently than in the Early English style. Three examples are given, PL. XI. fig. 2, from Yaxley, Hunts, very early in the style, as appears by the abacus, PL. XII. fig. 9, and the annexed cut, from Harringworth, Northants.

The neck, or astragal, forms an important detail in determining the dates of capitals. In the Early English it is usually a heavy and bold annular molding, of a stilted or oval shape, or rather more than half a circle, as PL. X. fig. 11. Either this or the semi-hexagon (fig. 15) is the prevailing form. The Decorated neck is almost always the scroll-molding; but both the Early English forms, with many others, will be found to occur. The capitals of both styles are often so nearly identical in general character and principles of formation, that a practised eye may now and then be deceived in their date. And it is here important to remark, that though the vast majority of capitals in all English buildings will be found to fall in with the rules laid down in this work, anomalies do occur which present difficulties in any attempt to classify them; and the same is true of bases.

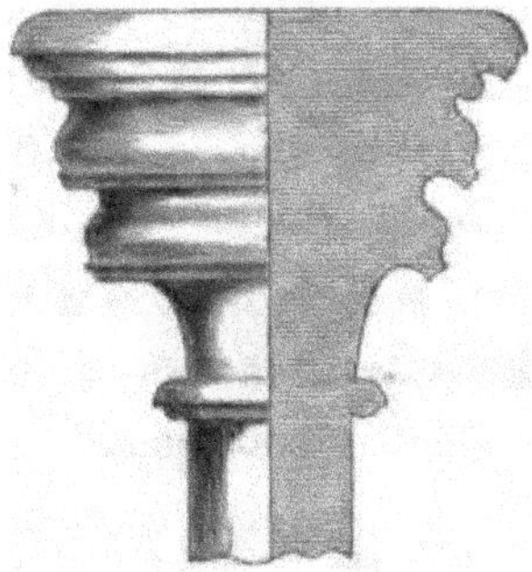

Harringworth.

Perpendicular capitals present very marked features, which are seldom liable to be mistaken. The moldings are large, angular, meagre, and few. Neither abacus nor bell is clearly defined—a fact similar to that already stated with regard to the arch-moldings of this style, that the distinction of *orders* is generally lost. The abacus, in short, no longer appears as a separable member, and the bell either wholly vanishes or is very imperfectly developed. The upper part of the abacus is usually sloped off to a sharp edge, like the chamfer of an angle; the section of the molding below resembles the letter S, being an ogee formed by a bold concave returning into a prominent convex (as at Coton); and, above all, the capital is nearly always *octagonal*, while that of the preceding styles is commonly round. The shaft, however, is circular in Perpendicular work; while octagonal capitals only occur in the other styles in the case of large single columns of the same shape, if we except a few cases of Early English arcading shafts with octagonal capitals, as in the transepts at Histon, near Cambridge, the west front of Peterborough Cathedral, and in the choir-aisle of Fountains Abbey.

Coton, Camb.

The same principle which induced the later architects to prefer sharp edges and abrupt lines in their moldings to the soft and blending Decorated forms, made them revert to the octagonal capital to the rejection of the circular. The base, however, is generally circular in its upper members, and octagonal below, as in PL. XV. figs. 1 and 2.

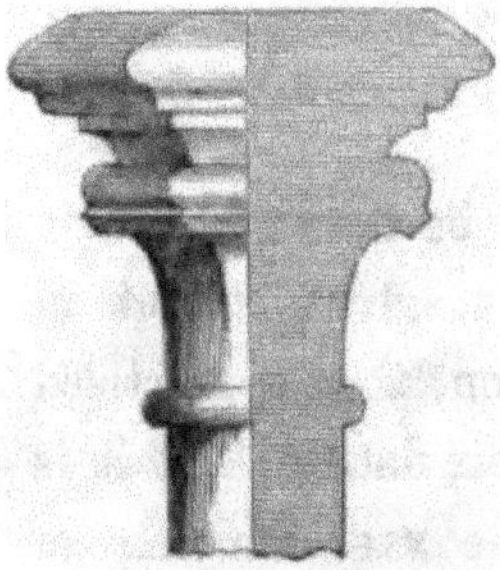

Lancaster Church.

Perpendicular capitals are often embattled, as PL. XII. figs. 16, 22, 26, 29, an arrangement which is rare in the preceding style.

The astragal, or neck, is either a plain round or a kind of debased scroll-molding with the upper edge chamfered, as in the abacus. Another form, resembling a coarse keel-mold, common to both members, is that shown in PL. VIII. fig. 21, which occurs in the abacus of PL. XIII. fig. 8, and the neck of fig. 15.

The bell with its overhanging and undercut moldings having vanished, the projection of the capital is produced by a meagre slope, as figs. 3 and 5. Sometimes, however, but not very often, the bell remains. Its form seems capricious, and reducible to no certain rule, though the profile is often much the same as in Decorated work. Perhaps greater license was taken in general in designing the moldings of this style than in any other.

The section of the Perpendicular abacus is a mere corruption of the Decorated scroll-molding. Thus in PL. XIII. figs. 7, 10, and 12, we see nearly the same form as in the Decorated; and by omitting the under roll, as in figs. 20, 21, we obtain the ordinary profile of fig. 15. This debasement of the scroll-molding is separately shown in PL. IV. fig. 22.

It will not be necessary to occupy much space in stating the places from which our numerous sections of capitals and bases are taken. A few only of the most remarkable shall be thus specified. PL. X. figs. 7, 8, are from Frieston, Lincolnshire. Here the bell is of rather unusual form, perhaps more so in this than in the next style, as in PL. XI. figs. 9, 11, 15, 16, 17. PL. X. fig. 9, is a noble capital from Stickney, Lincolnshire, late in the style, as appears from the undercut scroll-abacus. Fig. 10 is from the same place. Of the same date and character are 12 and 13; the former from Lincoln Cathedral, the latter from Ruskington. Fig. 18 is from the Chapter House of Furness Abbey, and has the double bell; fig. 19 from Tintern Abbey, very rich and fine in its profile.* Fig. 22 is shown in elevation, by studying which, those who are unacquainted with the details of the styles may form a correct idea of the leading characteristics of the capitals of this period. It is from Furness Abbey. Figs. 23, 24, 26, are from Bolton Abbey. Fig. 28 is from Tintern, rather late, and remarkable in its profile. Fig. 29 is from Arreton, Isle of Wight. Fig. 30 from

* The student is again referred to Potter's illustrations of this abbey for many beautiful capitals and bases, drawn on a large scale.

Saffron Walden, of much larger size than usual. Fig. 37 is from Bolton Abbey, with the nail-head in the hollow above the bell. Fig. 40 is the elevation of the most ordinary form in shafts and clustered piers.

PL. XI. figs. 1 and 2, are from Yaxley; fig. 4 is a fine capital of very unusual size and depth, in a chapel used as the vestry in the church at Boston. Fig. 3 is from Fletton, Hunts; figs. 6, 7, from Leverton; fig. 9 from Sibsey; fig. 10 from Stickford; fig. 11 from Partney—all in Lincolnshire. Fig. 12 is from Legburn, in the same county, of large size (15 inches in depth); fig. 13 from Waltham. Figs. 15, 16, 17, are all from Lincolnshire, and almost identical. This is the form of the pier-capitals at Heckington. Fig. 18 is from Aswardby, Lincolnshire, depth one foot; fig. 22 is from Abington, Cambridgeshire.

The sections of Decorated capitals in PL. XII. are mostly from churches in the neighbourhood of Cambridge. Fig. 14 is not uncommon in Transition to Perpendicular; it occurs at Maxey, Northamptonshire, and at Louth (see PL. XI. fig. 28). Fig. 13 is from a fine monument at Little Shelford, near Cambridge. The rest of the sections in this plate are Perpendicular.

Willingham, Cambridge.

PL. XII. fig. 16, is from Careby, Lincolnshire. This has a battlement above, and the double ogee below, the abacus. A similar feature is the wave-molding, in the same position, in the Decorated capitals of the nave columns at Dunchurch, Warwickshire.

PL. XII. fig. 19, is from Uffington, near Stamford. This and the next illustrate the methods of obtaining the *plane* of the moldings, which in this style should be attended to. Figs. 22, 23, 24, are from St. Martin's, figs. 26 and 27 from St. John's, fig. 28 from St. George's, and fig. 29 from the Bede House, all in Stamford.

PL. XIII. fig. 1, is from Long Melford, Suffolk; fig. 4 from Louth; figs. 8, 9, 12, from Colchester; fig. 14 from Harston, near Cambridge; fig. 13 from Fen Ditton; fig. 17 from Mattishall, Norfolk. Here the abacus is octagonal, the bell and neck circular. Fig. 18 is from Elsworth Hall,* Norfolk; fig. 16 from Dry Drayton, near Cambridge; fig. 19 from Saham Toney.

SECTION X.

OF BASES.

THE earliest examples of bases must be looked for in the rude monolith blocks which support the pillars or pilasters in the Ante-Norman churches, such as at Wittering, near Stamford, and others already mentioned. These are often mere shapeless lumps, laid down as they were raised from the quarry, and consisting only of the single member thus presented to view. Norman architecture first adopted a more regular method in constructing the footing of a column, and from that arrangement those of the subsequent styles are readily deduced. The Classic pillar was evidently the prototype of all these.

Bases consist, in early work, of at least two distinct members—the *plinth*, or lower step, of solid masonry, generally square in early work, but octagonal in later; and the *base-moldings*, a series of annular rolls, slopes, or hollows, taking the form of the column, and forming an ornamental junction between the shaft and its essential constructive member, the plinth. In Decorated and Perpendicular columns, the plinth is usually divided into heights, stages, or *tables*, by gradually

* An interesting specimen, very little known, of a moated mansion of the Fifteenth Century.

spreading courses, each separated from the next by a plain or molded chamfer.

Of Norman bases it is not necessary to treat at length. The varieties of form are not numerous; and as they do not involve complex moldings, like the after styles, it will be sufficient to direct the attention of the student to the upper members, in which the character of a base may be said principally to consist. In shafts, the base often resembles the capital inverted; in some instances, the one might be substituted for the other with scarcely any perceptible change of appearance. Often a bold annular roll, quirked on the under side (as seen in PL. XIV. figs. 3, 7), divides the shaft from the plinth. PL. XXI. fig. 9, is from Fountains Abbey. Fig. 10 is a little later, from the Chapter House of the same place. A very common form is shown in PL. XIV. fig. 8, from the nave of Peterborough Cathedral. This occurs in St. Sepulchre's, Cambridge, where the present bases were cut from a very small piece, only a few inches wide, which alone remained in the eight massive columns of the circular part.

The moldings of the earliest Norman bases are frequently "little better than scratches upon the surface,"* and generally consist of two reverse curves, a concave above and a convex below. Nothing approaching to developed isolated members and distinct gradations was known in the early part of the twelfth century.

St. Sepulchre, Cambridge.

Helmsley Ch., Yorkshire.

St. Mary's, Huntingdon.

A little before the Transition period, a modification (often with very trifling departure from the Classic) of the Attic base was introduced, from which the Early English is directly derived. The Attic base is given in PL. XIV. figs. 1 and 2. It consists of two rounds, with an intervening hollow separated from them

* Willis's Canterbury, p. 76.

by fillets. If we compare this form with some of the early Italian-Gothic bases, figs. 3, 4,* and with one from Canterbury Cathedral† (date about 1180), fig. 5, we shall find them rather identical with than similar to the Classic. The uppermost fillet, or first member at the lower extremity of the shaft, was, however, omitted in most if not in all cases; and the form in fig. 7, from Peterborough Cathedral, was very much in vogue.‡ This example leads us at once to the ordinary Early English base (fig. 12), the chief peculiarity of which consists in the intermediate hollow being cut *downwards* rather than *sideways*, and extended from half to three-quarters of a circle, so that it is capable of containing water, which may often be observed standing in exterior bases. The filleted rolls on each side, above and below the hollow, are naturally formed by cutting off the feather edges seen in fig. 3. A valuable example of the Transition base is fig. 6, taken from the great central piers of Byland Abbey, shortly after some extensive excavations had revealed a great part of the ground-plan and lower portions of the columns of that once splendid church. Here we most distinctly recognize the peculiar feature of the Attic base, the *side-hollow* of fig. 1—the lateral semicircle in place of the descending three-quarter circle. It must be particularly remembered that this water-holding base is contemporary with the first dawn of the Transition style, and may commonly be met with in pointed Norman work, *i. e.* as early as 1160 or 1170. It is found in the Transition work of William of Sens at Canterbury.§

There are two kinds of Early English bases. The first, and

* From Willis's Architecture of the Middle Ages.

† Canterbury Cathedral has a very French character in the work of William of Sens, and this is more like Classic work than English architecture generally.

‡ The bases of the pointed Norman columns in the nave of Buildwas Abbey are nearly identical with this.—See Potter, PL. X.

§ Willis's Canterbury, p. 76.

by far the most common, is the form given in PL. XIV. fig. 12; the other seems to be derived either from omitting the hollow altogether, as in figs. 10, 11, and thus bringing the rolls into contact, or from supplying its place by another similar roll, as fig. 15, or even by an interposed square edge, or *plinthiform* member, as fig. 9, the bases of the choir columns in Rivaulx Abbey. Generally, this intermediate roll is rather smaller, and often a little depressed inwardly, as fig. 16, from Ely. This base occurs almost invariably in Westminster Abbey. It is seldom found except in the more advanced or florid period of the Early English, when geometric windows of two or more lights had begun to supersede the single lancet. Hence was at once derived the ordinary Decorated base, figs. 33, 34, 35.

In very rich Early English bases there are often double hollows between filleted rolls—after the analogy of the double row of moldings to the bell in capitals. And below these, at some distance, occur other series of very bold annular rolls, single, double, or even triple. PL. XIV. fig. 18, is the base of a great pier in Lincoln Cathedral. Fig. 26, from the beautiful Galilee at Ely, where the bases are worked out of hard Purbeck marble, and have all been elaborately polished. Fig. 27 is from Skelton, near York.

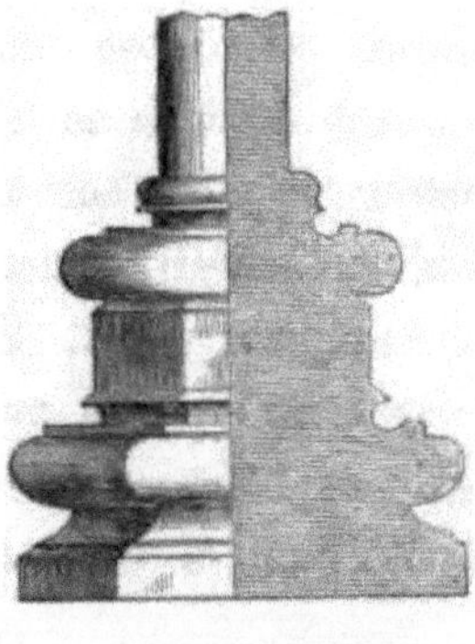

Peterborough Cathedral.

PL. XXI. fig. 4, is an example, of the most ordinary form, from the revestry or chapter-room at Ripon Cathedral. Fig. 7 is from York Cathedral.

Sometimes the fillet is omitted in the upper roll, as PL. XIV. fig. 25. In fig. 20, the hollow again approaches that of the Attic base. Fig. 18, from Lincoln Cathedral, is a fine piece of detail, of great richness and considerable spread. Fig. 30, from

Furness Abbey, is remarkable for the omission of the hollow in the upper member. The examples given in elevation, figs. 28 and 29, the former from Tintern, the latter from Furness Abbey, will convey a correct idea of the general appearance.* The spread of the base generally equals that of the capital, or nearly so.

There is something extremely elegant in the form of this, the more usual kind of Early English base; and it is, moreover, surprising to notice the uniformity which everywhere prevails both in it and the capital of this period. The plainer form (figs. 10, 11, 15, 16, 17, 21) may possibly have gradually superseded the more elaborate, either from the difficult and complex work of the latter, or because the hollow was externally apt to be filled up with standing water, moss, or earth, and internally with dust and dirt, as it will almost invariably be found to be. Probably the desire of forming a better weathering had much influence in the change.

In Early English bases it is also to be remarked that the large spreading roll, which forms the lower of the two members between which the deep hollow is placed, is worked out of the block, with which it usually stands *flush*, or in the same plane, by a quirk or angular nook. This is almost invariable; and it is mentioned particularly with reference to Decorated bases, where a marked difference in this part is observable. Here we usually find either the scroll-molding (fig. 35, from Coton, near Cambridge) or a flat under-edge, as fig. 42, from the nave-piers at Trumpington; or the part of the base below it cut away, so that it overhangs clear, as fig. 40, the base of the beautiful central column in the Chapter House at Wells; fig. 39, from the doorway in the same place; fig. 37, from St. Mary's Abbey, York. Fig. 45, from Fishtoft, Lincolnshire. This is generally a mark of late or florid Early English, when found in work of the

* The engraving is slightly incorrect, from the shaft not standing true in the centre.

thirteenth century, as PL. XXI. fig. 5, an elegant base from the library of York Cathedral.

One of the commonest Decorated bases is that shown in PL. XIV. fig. 35; the number of rolls being generally three, but often only two, as fig. 34. In fig. 39 there are four; but the uppermost is of lead, by which the shaft is fastened. Not a few modifications of this form occur; but they are seldom very complex. Fig. 43 is from the nave-pillars at Bottisham, near Cambridge; fig. 38 is from the arcade in the Lady Chapel at Ely, worked in Purbeck marble. Here the lower member is the roll-and-fillet, which is not uncommon. It is partially developed in fig. 41, from Over and Histon; an example which retains a singular trace in its upper member of the side hollow of the Attic base. PL. XV. fig. 3, is of unusual profile; it is from the chancel at Over, Transition to Perpendicular. PL. XIV. fig. 33, is from the nave-piers at Tintern—already noticed as a specimen of the inverted scroll-molding. Fig. 44 is from Boston. This form is not unusual late in the style.

Decorated bases are often stilted, or raised above the floor, with the plinth formed by graduated stages or tables, as before described. This principle was carried to an extravagant excess in the next style; in some instances, as those under the western tower at Ely, the uppermost member stands six or even eight feet from the ground. The lower part of Decorated bases is sometimes octagonal, or polygonal, as in the columns which support the octagon at Ely; and sometimes these faces are fluted or hollow-chamfered. In the Decorated columns supporting the vault of the Lady Chapel at Wells, the base-moldings are raised a considerable height from the floor. In the choir at the Temple Church (1240), the principle of stilting the bases may be seen, the plinth being very large and high, and the moldings approximating to the Decorated profile.

Instead of the three half-rounds which ordinarily constitute the Decorated base, one member, generally the second, but often the first, is sometimes, as it were, scooped out in the middle, in what might be called the inverted wave-molding, so as to form an ogee curvature. This is seen in PL. XIV. figs. 36 (from the Lady Chapel, Ely), 40, and 42. Hence the bell-shaped base of the next style (PL. XV. figs. 1 and 2) was immediately derived. Compare PL. XXI. fig. 6, a Decorated base from the nave of York Cathedral, with fig. 8, a Perpendicular base from Ripon Cathedral. The sharp under edge of the second member in the former example is a peculiar feature, decisive of Decorated work.

So similar, however, are the two forms, that some pure Decorated bases may occasionally be found which would have been equally correct in a Perpendicular column. This ogee curve seems to be derived from the several rolls which we have seen were used in the bases, being a natural variation to avoid repetition. It does not appear to occur in early, or geometric Decorated.

But few examples of Decorated bases have been given, because any important varieties from the forms described are not of sufficiently frequent occurrence to render it necessary to illustrate them. They are very chaste and elegant in profile; often standing but a little above the floor-line, especially in shafts, and thus of modest and unpretending contour. They are for the most part of decided character; and where any difficulty occurs in determining their date, an inspection of the capital, according to the rules already laid down, will readily remove it.

The bases of Perpendicular columns are various; but rather in degrees of richness and the number of graduations than in difference of form in the principal members. The prevailing characteristic is a large bell-shaped spread in the upper part, often resting on a cushion-like member, and forming with it the contour of a double ogee in section. PL. XV. figs. 1 and 2, are from Crosby Hall, and give a correct representation of the most ordinary kind. It will be particularly observed that the lower part is almost invariably octagonal, the upper being generally round, though sometimes, as the capital always is, octagonal. From the great size and height of the best examples they are not so easily engraved in a small space: PL. XV., however, contains enough specimens to guide the student under ordinary circumstances. Fig. 5 is from Louth; fig. 13 from All Saints', Stamford; fig. 17 from Haslingfield; fig. 18 from Holy Trinity, Colchester; fig. 20 from St. Edward's, Cambridge; fig. 21 from Herne, Kent.

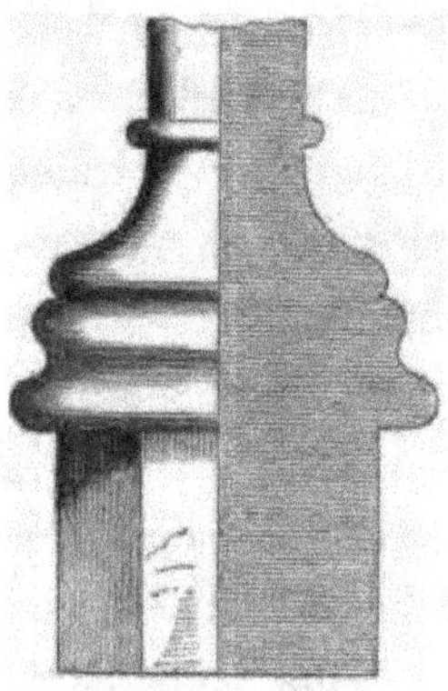

Lancaster.

Almost every Perpendicular base has either one or more stages, sloping off by a hollow *ledgement* or chamfer, as figs. 15, 16, 17; or by a second bell-shaped slope, as figs. 5, 6, 14. The ancient name for the lower member was the *ground-table* * (especially when applied to mural basement moldings). All Perpendicular bases have an annular roll, resembling the neck of capitals, for the uppermost member. This is often the debased roll-and-fillet shown in PL. VIII. fig. 21, as in PL. XV. fig. 15, or the debased scroll-molding, as in PL. XV. fig. 18. This feature is almost invariable, and is not found in the same isolated form in any other style.

It is singular that edge lines occur less in Perpendicular than in any other bases, almost every point being carefully rounded off. There is a peculiar nakedness in the straight unbroken line of the *lower*, or *ground-table*, rising, as it does, abruptly from the floor to the height of two feet and more, as in the interior of King's College Chapel; but the bell is of remarkably graceful form, and perhaps few will prefer the

* See Willis's Architectural Nomenclature, § 39.

contour of PL. XIV. fig. 29 or 32, to that of PL. XV. figs. 1 and 2.

Fig. 4 is from the Lady Chapel, Peterborough; fig. 6 from Carbrook; fig. 7 from Saham; fig. 8 from Dereham; fig. 9 from Norwich Cathedral; fig. 10 from Mattishall; fig. 11 from Swanton Morley,—all in Norfolk; figs. 12, 15, from Colchester; fig. 14 from St. John's, Stamford; fig. 16 from St. Alban's; fig. 22 from Saffron Walden.

SECTION XI.

OF HOOD-MOLDINGS AND STRING-COURSES.

THIS is by no means an unimportant branch of the study of Gothic Moldings, the varieties and peculiar characteristics of the styles being as well defined in such details as in any hitherto described. Of the immense diversity of forms only some of the most ordinary can be enumerated; for capricious irregularities constantly occur, which, as they seem reducible to no certain rule, hardly claim a place in laying down the principles of a system. Yet, though the *form* may be arbitrary, the *character* is generally maintained.

PL. XVI. contains a series of moldings of this sort (for hood-moldings and string-courses must be classed together, being in fact very often identical, or the one continued from the other), divided into three parts, illustrating the three styles.

It has been before observed that string-courses may be regarded as the successors of the horizontal lines by which Classical is principally distinguished from Gothic architecture; and the importance of them will be felt when it is remembered that all masonry is made up of successive layers, so that they

Fig. 43 is from the vestibule of the Chapter House at Wells, early in the style. Fig. 50 is from Over, near Cambridge; fig. 45 from Bottisham.

The rounded form of the upper side, or weathering, is characteristic of the first two styles; the angular or chamfered of the last—although this peculiarity is also very common in late Decorated buildings. In this respect also string-courses follow the principle of the abacus of capitals.* PL. XVI. figs. 52 and 55, may therefore be pronounced late in the style. Undercuttings, it has already been remarked, occur principally in the time of Edwards I. and II., as figs. 32, 44, 51.

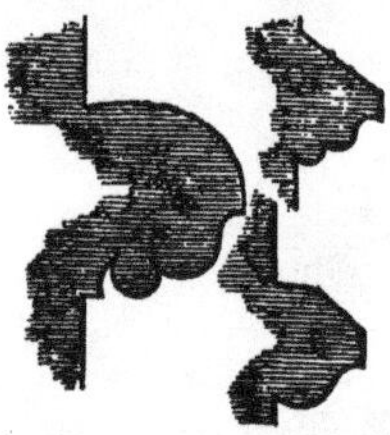

Transition Strings.

Perpendicular strings and hood-moldings are generally marked by the sloping plane of the upper surface, as PL. XVI. figs. 60, 61. The details of the parts underneath are so varied as to render it almost impossible to give anything like a complete account of them; yet, numerous as they are, they will generally be found to recur with tolerable uniformity. Usually there is a small bowtell in the lowest part, as in figs. 57, 59, 62, 64, 68, 71, and others, more or less clearly developed. This is rather a characteristic mark of the style. PL. XX. fig. 16, from Grantham Church, is another example. Fig. 18 is a string-course from the same place. Perhaps the most ordinary forms are PL. XVI., figs. 61, 68, 71. The double ogee, as fig. 60, and the combination of the ogee with the under fillet, already described, as in figs. 56, 77, often occur. Fig. 78 exhibits the peculiar Perpendicular form already pointed out. A semicircle sunk in the under side of half a square projecting

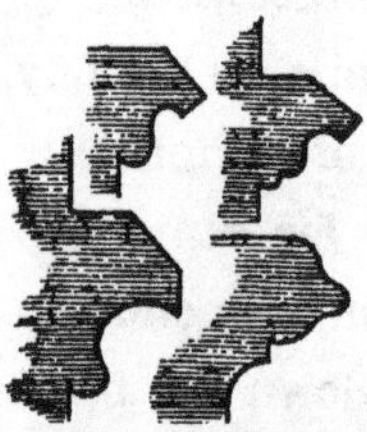

Perpendicular Strings.

* Early English strings are often continued from the abaci of capitals, which perhaps accounts for this fact.

diagonally, as in fig. 66, is also a common variety. Embattled string-courses occur now and then in this style, as in the cornice of the aisles at Cromer Church, Norfolk.

In copying string-courses, it is better to draw the parts of the wall above and below perpendicularly on the paper, not only for a guide to show the direction of inclination or projection, which, without this, is left quite indefinite, but also because the wall often recedes above the string, or even overhangs, as fig. 56. The angles of the chamfers can best be attained by bending a piece of lead across them. Sometimes a foot-rule may be bent against the wall and the under part, as fig. 67, and thus the exact angle can readily be transferred to paper.

Much more might, and indeed ought, to be said on the subject of moldings, were it the intention of the writer to attempt anything like a *complete* essay. For example, there yet remain wholly unnoticed several important cases of the application of moldings in Gothic architecture. Basements, weatherings of buttresses, cappings of parapets and battlements, plans of monials, groin-ribs, timbers of roofs, and other wood-work, besides the many and interesting varieties of ornamental or floriated moldings, are all well deserving of the closest attention. But *a great book is a great evil,* as a philosopher of old has declared; and it has been the wish of the author rather to win the attention of the reader, by pointing out the way to copy and observe, than to deter him by the uninviting form of a grave and heavy book. Quite enough has been said, it is conceived, to illustrate the really essential principles of the science. And no one need feel any difficulty or perplexity in recognizing the details of the styles, who will take the trouble to apply the rules laid down in this little work.

Plate I.

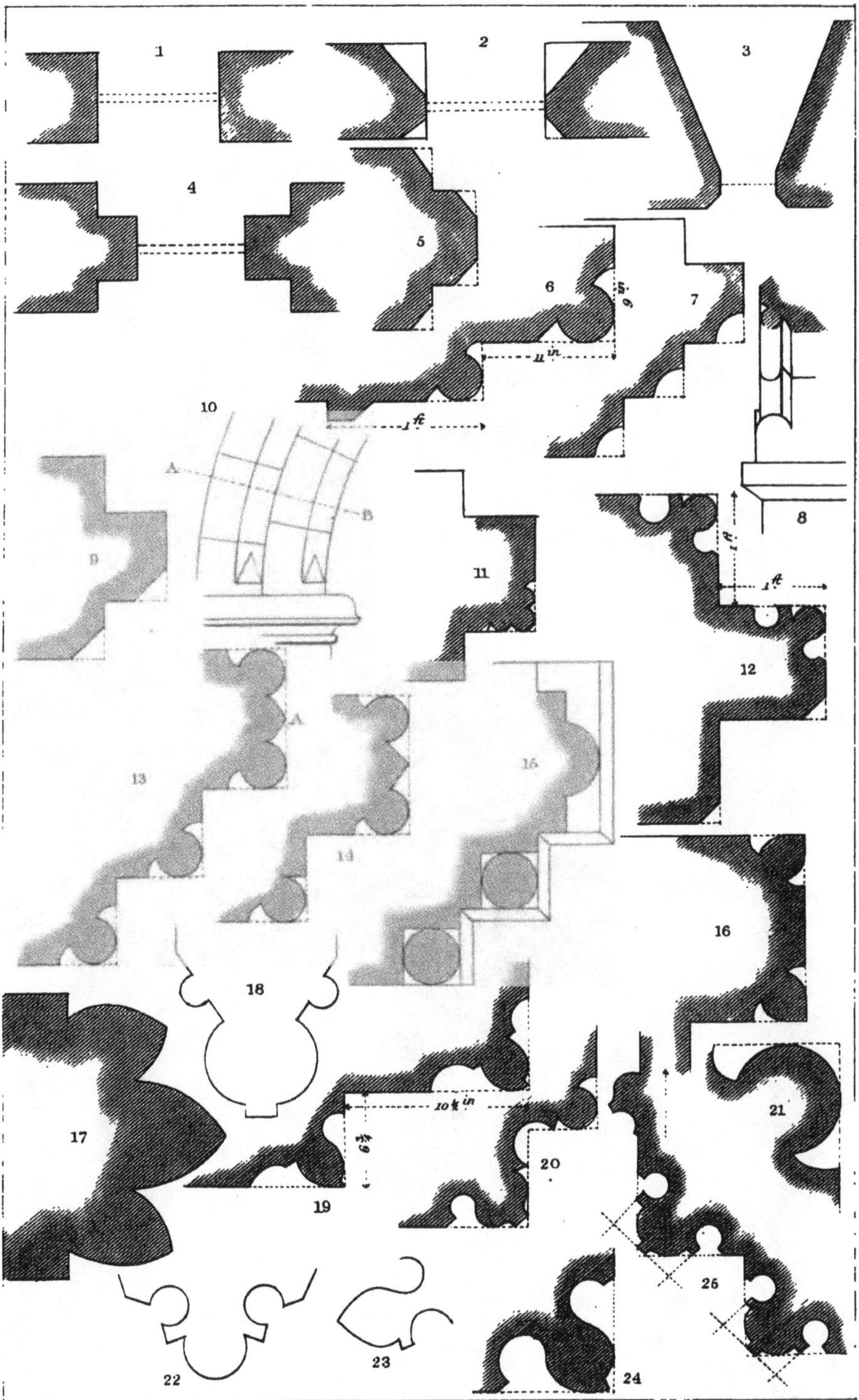

J. H. Le Keux sc.

PLATE II.

1. Middle Rasen—Early English Pier Arch.
2. Ludborough, Lincolnshire—Doorway.
3. Langtoft. do. Chancel Arch.
5. Great Grimsby, do. South Porch, Jamb.
6. Cherry Hinton, Cambridgeshire—North Door.
7. Do. do. Chancel Door, Interior.
8. Do. do. Pier Arch.
9. Over, do. Doorway.
10. Diagram of Planes—A Chamfer Plane.
    B Soffit Plane.
    C Wall Plane.
11. Over, Cambridgeshire.
13. Do. do. Window Jamb.
14. Madingley, do. do.
15. Stamford, All Saints'—Pier Arch.
16. Trumpington, Cambridgeshire—Doorway.
17. Tintern Abbey—Groin Rib.
18. Cambridge, St. Clement's—South Doorway.
19. Cherry Hinton—Inner Door, South Porch.

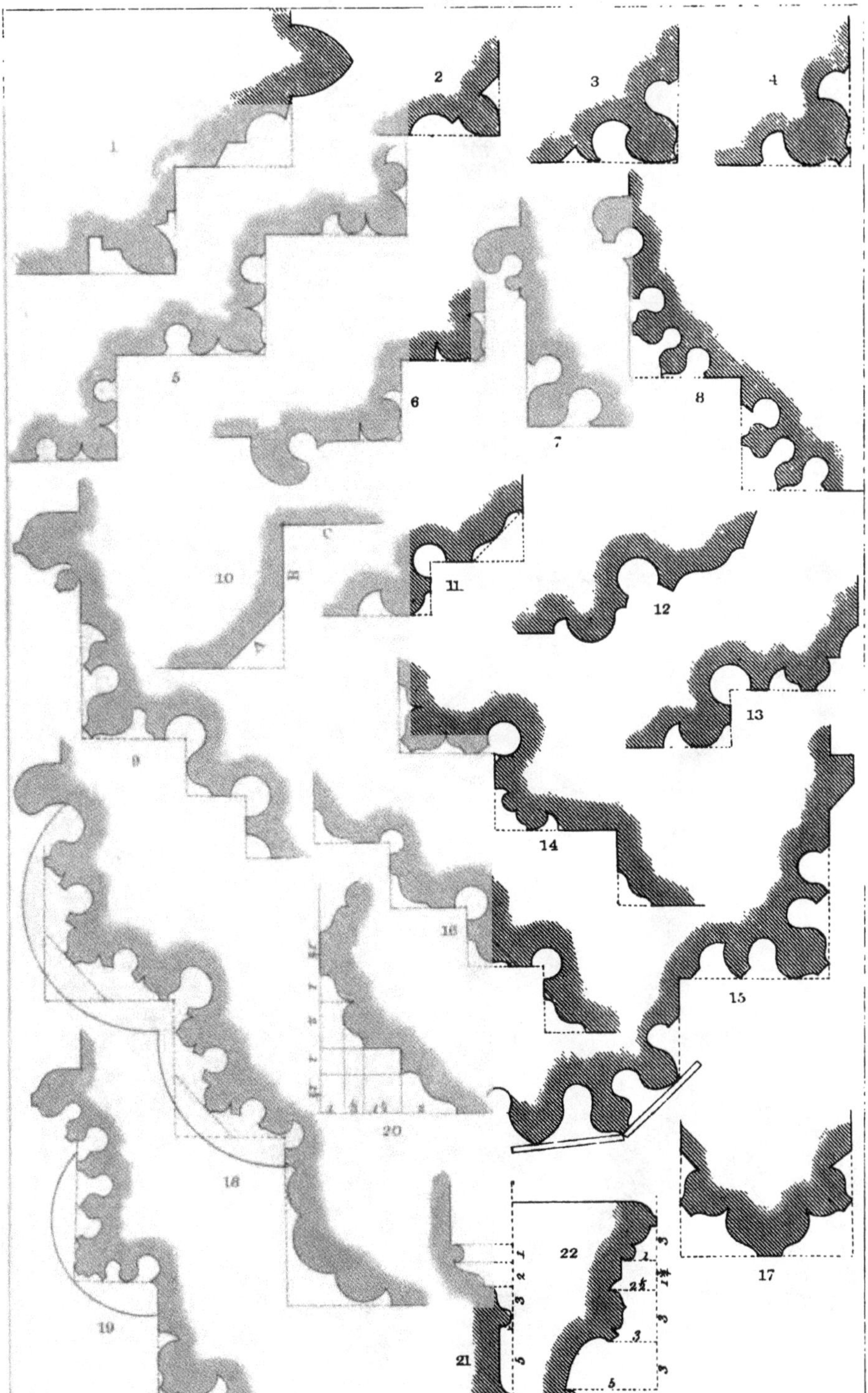

J. H. Le Keux, sc.

PLATE III.

1. Louth—Early English Doorway.
2. Plymouth—Belfry Arch.
3. Ely Cathedral—Pier Arches, Choir.
4. Robertsbridge Abbey—Groin Rib.
5. Tintern Abbey—Fragment.
6. St. Mary's Abbey, York—Fragment.
7. Robertsbridge Abbey—Groin Rib.
8. All Saints', Stamford.
9. Histon, Cambridgeshire—Arch over Piscina and Capital.
10. Wittering, Northants—Chancel Arch.
11. Furness Abbey—Chapter House.
12. St. Peter Gowts, Lincoln.
13. Ruskington, Lincolnshire.
14. Utterby, do.
15. Attleborough, Norfolk.
16. Common form of Decorated Pier.
17. Skelton, near York.
18. St. John's, Stamford.
19. St. Martin's, do.
20. St. Mary's, do.

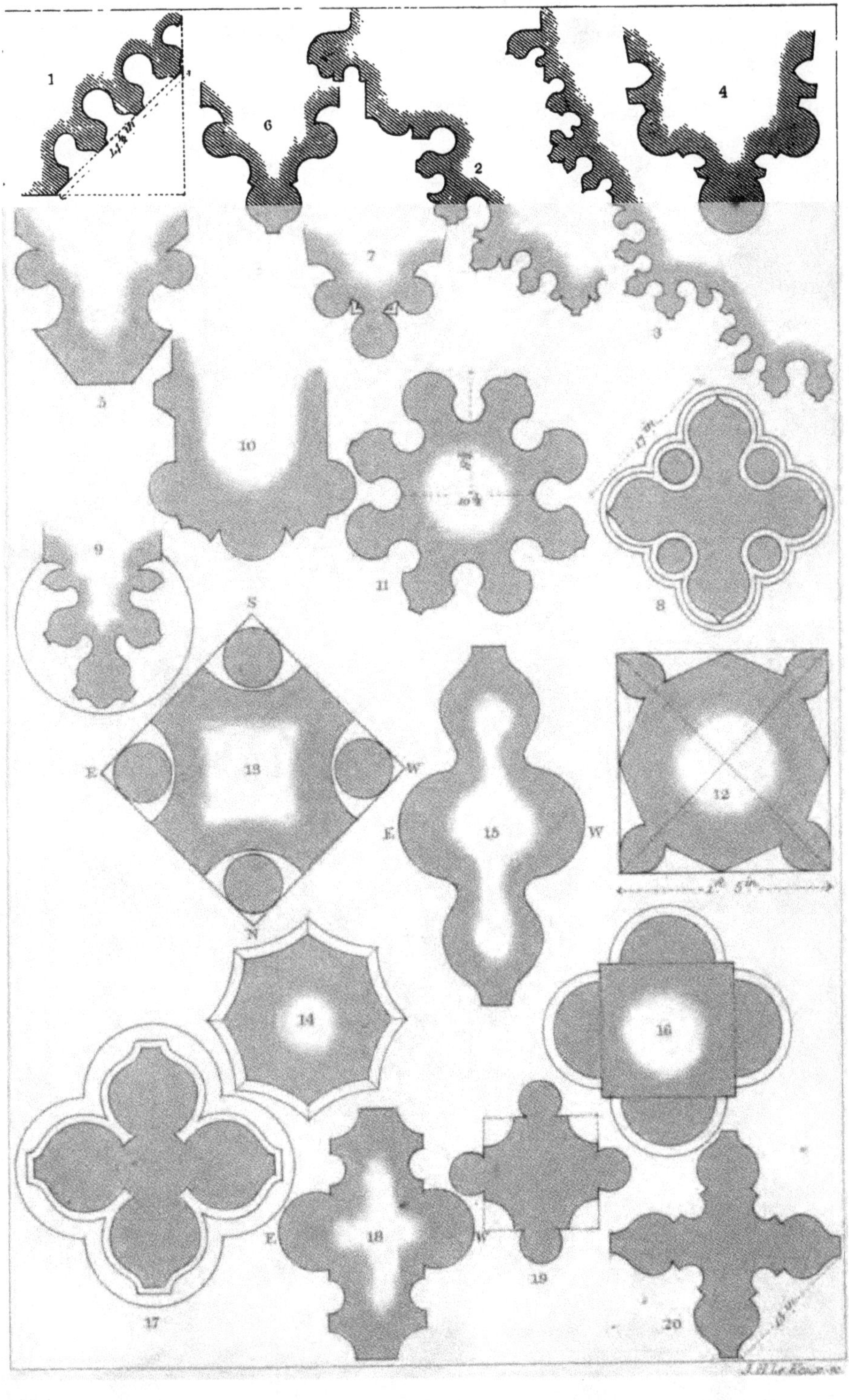

J. H. Le Keux sc.

PLATE IV.

1. Diagram of Roll Molding.
2. Reymerston, Norfolk.
3. Diagram of first sketch of Mold.
4. Barholme—semi-Norman Arch.
5. Barnack—Early English Arch.
6. Trumpington—Belfry Arch.
7. Glastonbury—c. 1200—Groin Rib.
8. Peterborough Cathedral—Groin Rib.
9. Diagram of possible first formation of Fillet.
10. Diagram of common form, Roll and Triple Fillet.
11. Ludborough, Lincolnshire—Chancel Doorway.
12.
13. } Lincoln Cathedral.
14. Yaxley, Hunts—Doorway.
15. Furness Abbey—Groin Rib.
16. Lincoln Cathedral—Arcade.
17. Diagram of Roll and Fillet.
18. Do. do.
19. Do. Broad Fillet.
20. Do. Scroll Molding.
21. Do. Fleur-de-lis Molding.
22. Do. variety of Scroll Molding.

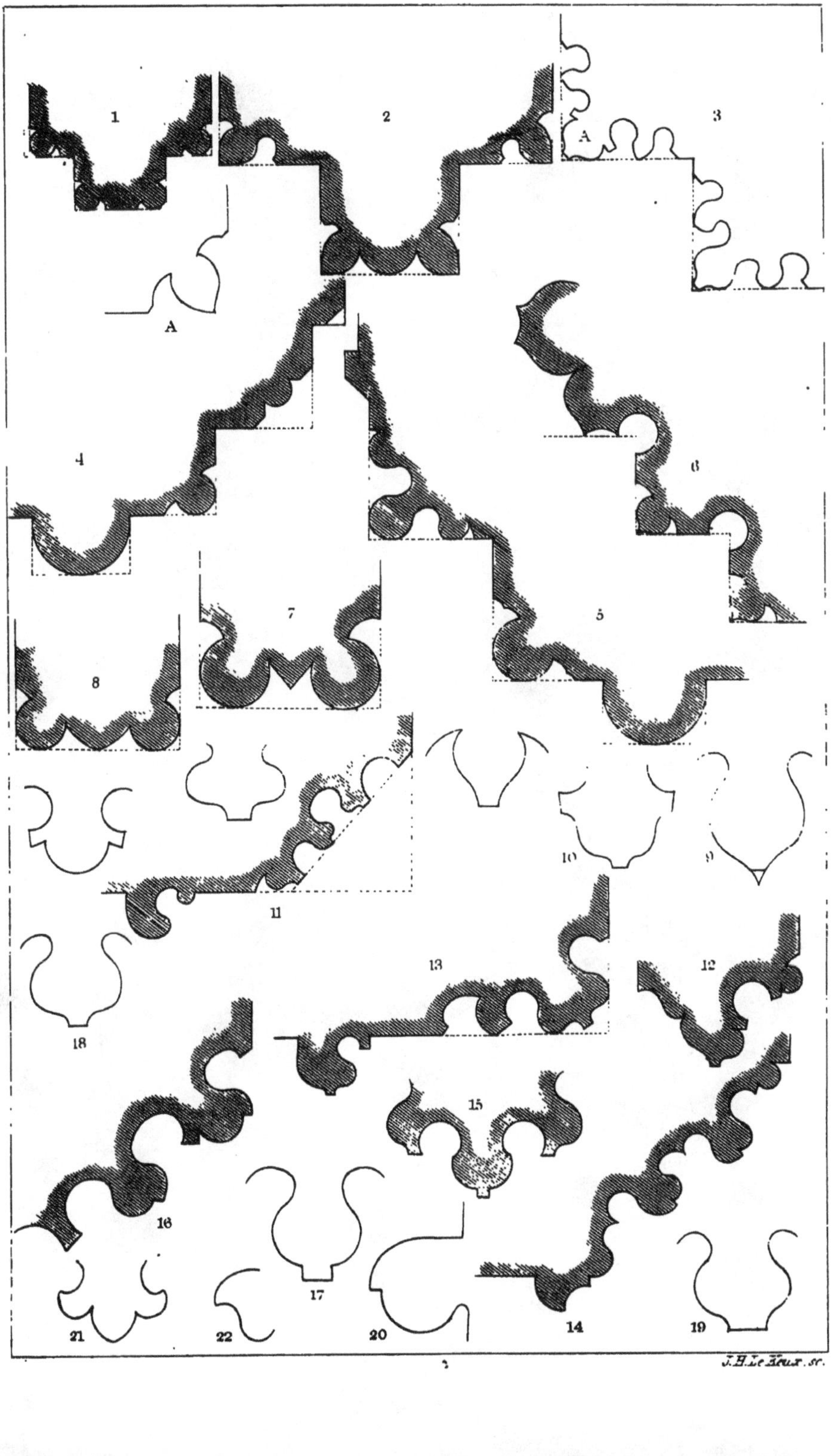

J. H. Le Keux. sc.

PLATE V.

1. Boston—Monument.
2. Great Ellingham—Doorway.
3. Attleborough, Norfolk—West Doorway.
4. Boston—Inner Doorway, South Porch.
5. Ewerby—Monument.
6. Northborough, Northants—Window Jamb.
7. Benington, Lincolnshire—Interior of Window Jamb.
8. Heckington, do. Interior of Window Jamb.
9. Do. do. Inner Jamb, East Window.
10. Benington, do. Exterior Jamb of Window.
11. Hingham, Norfolk—Chancel Doorway.
12. Attleborough—Doorway.
13. West Keal, Lincolnshire—Belfry Arch.
14. Hingham—Window.
15. Variety of Decorated Pier.
16. Streatham, Cambridgeshire.
17. Variety of Decorated Pier.

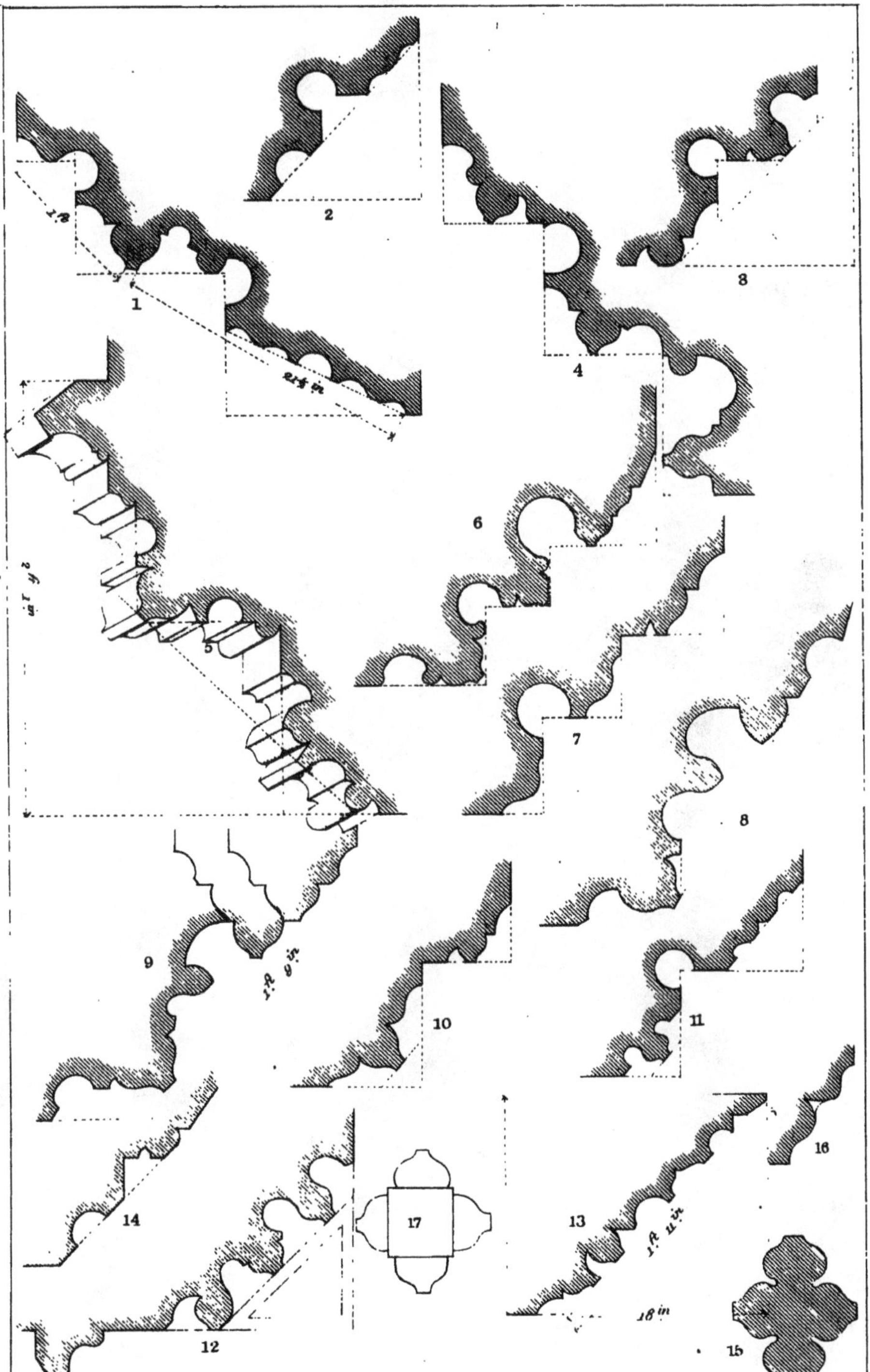

J. H. Le Keux, sc.

PLATE VI.

1. Little Ellingham, Norfolk—Doorway.
2. Hingham, Norfolk—West Door.
3. Do. do. Pier Arch.
4. Boston—Pier Arch.
5. Sleaford—Window Jamb.
6. Deopham—Doorway.
7. Boston—Monument in Church (A, Soffit).
8. Hingham—North Doorway.
9. Do. Double Ogee and Hollow.
10. Little Ellingham, Norfolk—Doorway.
11. Deopham—Inner Doorway, South Porch.
12. Benington, Lincolnshire—South Porch.
13. Hardingham, Norfolk—Archway.
14. Boston—East Window, Double Ogee and Hollow.
15. Stoke Golding, Leicestershire.

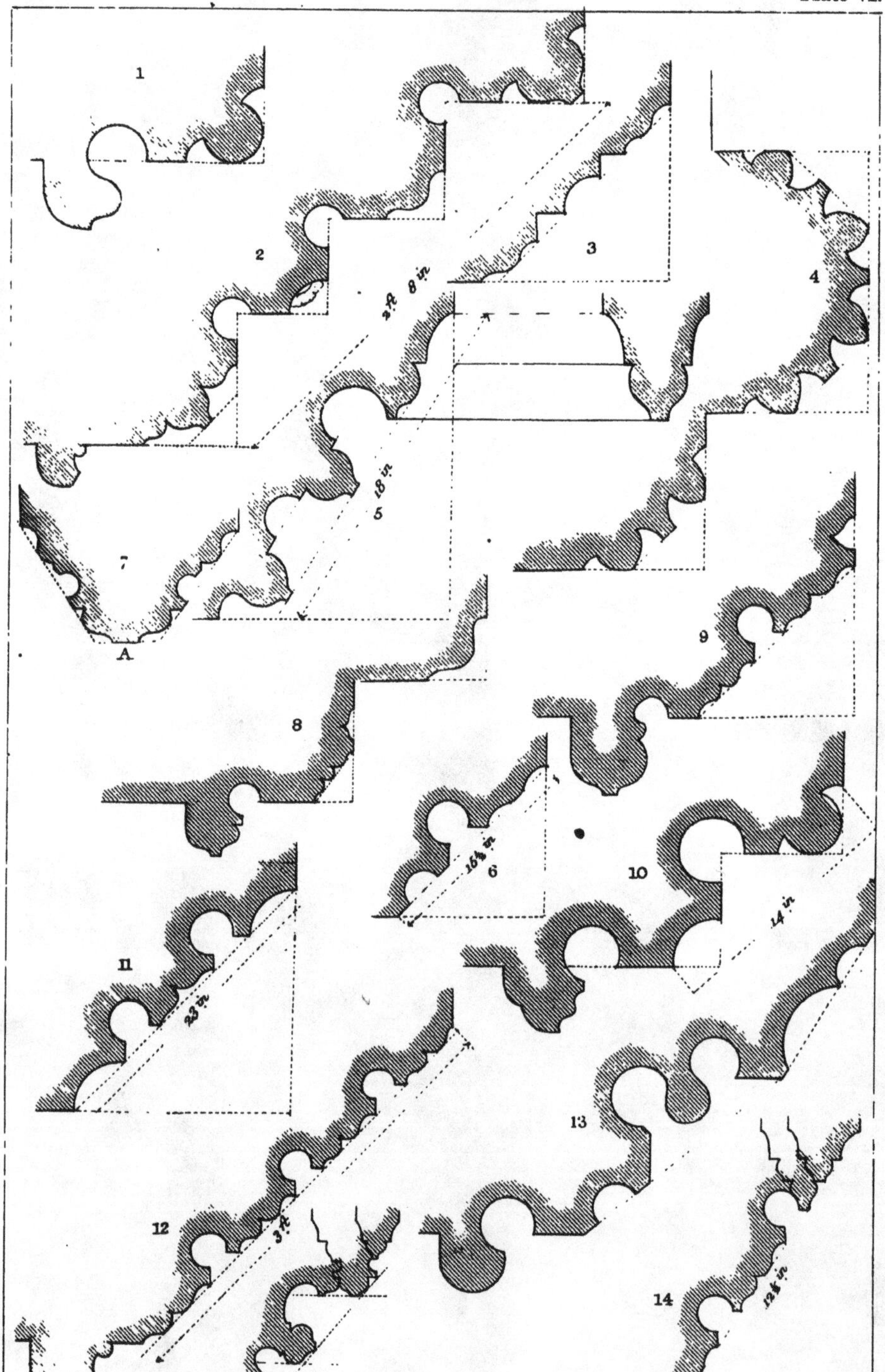
1
2
3
4
2 ft 8 in
18 in
5
7
A
8
9
6
16½ in
10
14 in
11
23 in
13
12
3 ft
15
14
12½ in

J. H. Le Keux, sc.

PLATE VII.

1. Llandaff Cathedral—West Doorway.
2. Diagram, Double Chamfer.
3. Trumpington—West Doorway.
4. Do. Pier Arch.
5. Rivaulx—Fragment.
6. Fen Stanton, Hunts—Window.
7. Northborough, Northants—Doorway.
8. Peterborough—Outer Archway, west entrance to precincts.
9. Yaxley, Hunts—Window.
10. Clipsham, Rutland.
11. Horbling, Lincolnshire.
12. Over, Cambridgshire—Window in Chancel.
13. Northborough—Outer Porch Doorway.
14. Rivaulx, Yorkshire—Fragment.
15. Do. do. Groin Rib.
16. West Keal—Doorway.
17. Wave Molds and Hollow.
18. Swanton Morley, Norfolk.
19. Hingham, do. Window.
20. Trumpington—East Window.
21. Keddington (or Ketton), Suffolk—Chancel Window.
22. Thurlby, Lincolnshire—Piscina.
23. Langtoft, Lincolnshire—South Doorway.
    - A Shallow Wave Mold.
    - B Sunken Chamfer.
    - C Deopham—Belfry Arch.

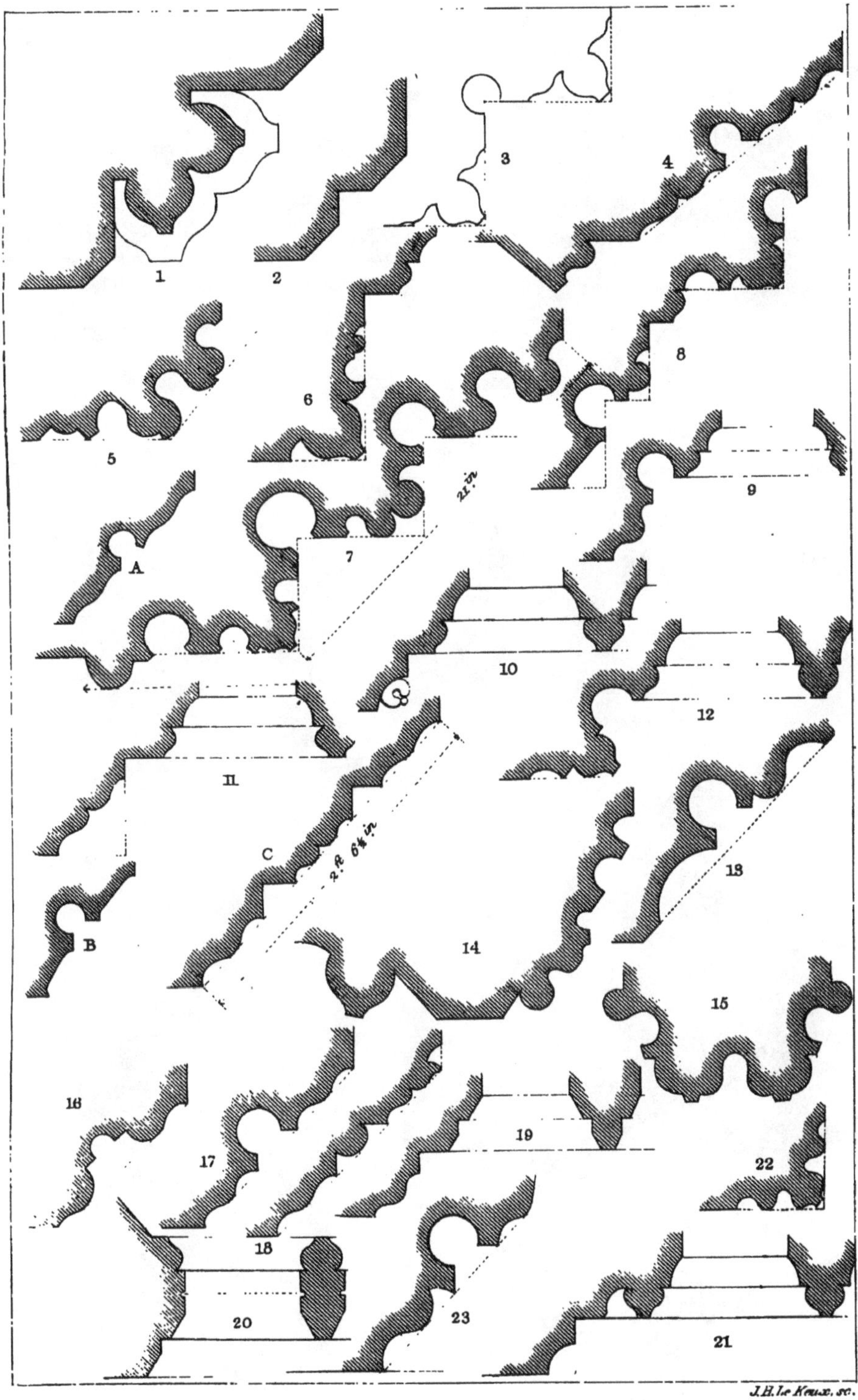
1
2
3
4
5
6
7
8
9
10
11
12
13
14
15
16
17
18
19
20
21
22
23
A
B
C
21 in
2 ft 6¼ in

J. H. Le Keux, sc.

PLATE VIII.

1. Uffington, near Stamford—West Doorway.
2. Dereham, Norfolk—West Doorway in isolated Tower.
3. Saham Toney, do.—West Doorway.
4. Fishtoft, Lincolnshire.
5. Leverton do. East Window.
6. Partney, do. Doorway.
7. Louth, do. Doorway.
8. Stewton, do. Window Jamb.
9. Lincoln—Oriel Window.
10. Chesterton, Cambridgeshire—East Window.
12. Lincoln Cathedral—South Choir Chapel.
13. St. Sepulchre's, Cambridge—Arch.
14. Great Gransden, near St. Neots, Hunts—Niche.
15. Stapleford, Cambridgeshire—East Window.
16. Great Shelford, do. Inner Doorway, South Porch.
17. Holy Trinity, Colchester—Pier Arch.
18. Long Melford, Suffolk—Pier Arch.
19. St. Martin's, Stamford—Doorway.
20. Do. do. Pier Arch.
21. Louth.

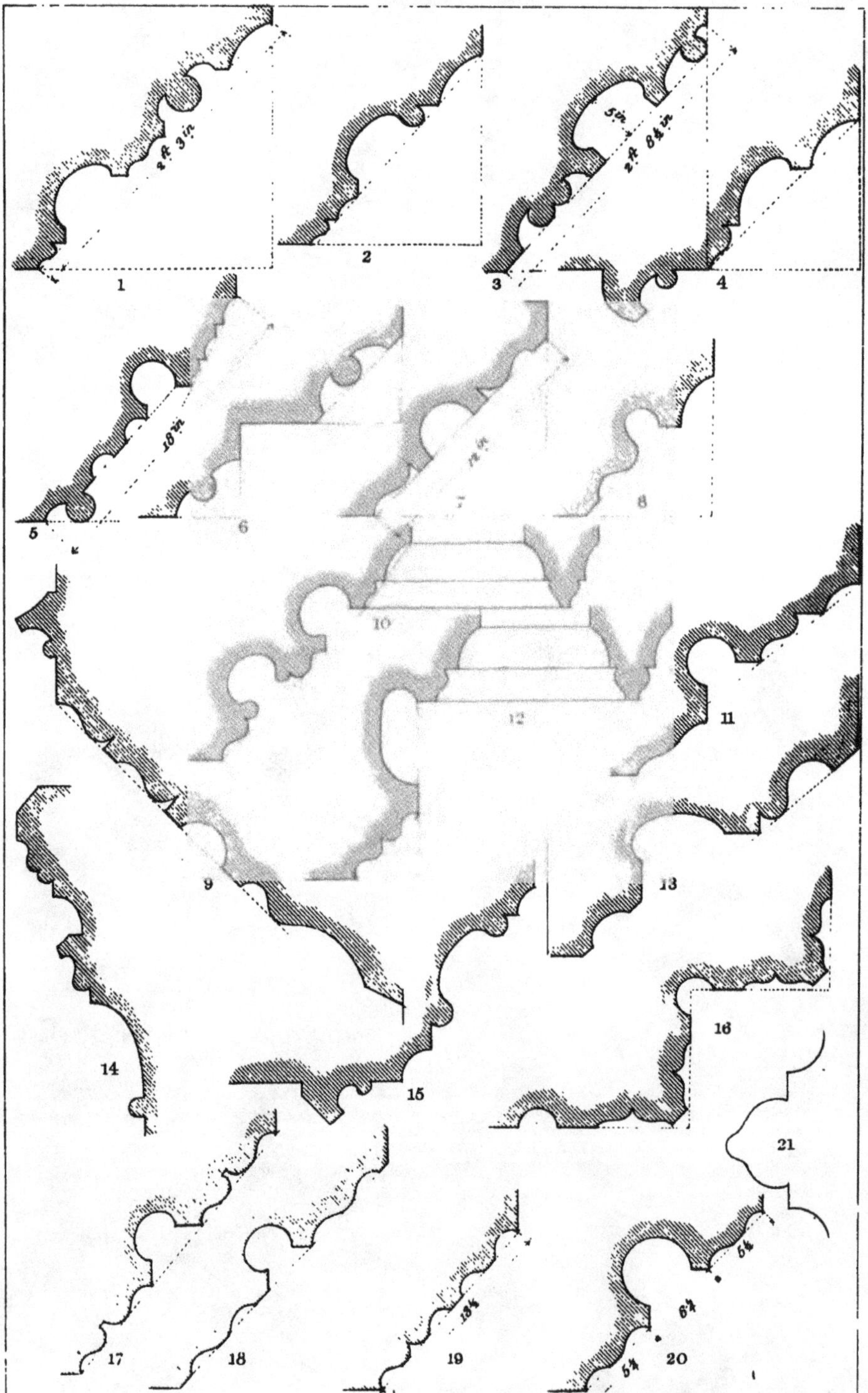
2 ft 3 in
1
2
5 in
2 ft 8¼ in
3
4
18 in
5
6
7
8
9
10
11
12
13
14
15
16
21
17
18
13¼
19
5¼
6¼
5¼
20

J. H. Le Keux, sc.

PLATE IX.

1. St. Martin's, Stamford—East Window.
2. Do. do. West Doorway.
3. St. John's, do. West Doorway.
4. Bede House, do.
5. All Saints', do. Pier Arch.
6. Do. do. West Doorway.
7. Histon, Cambridgeshire—Window.
8. Skirlaugh, Yorkshire—Chancel Doorway.
9. Harlton, Cambridgeshire—North Doorway.
10. Skirlaugh, Yorkshire—South Doorway.
11. Basingstoke, Hampshire.
12. Diagram of Window Jamb of common form.
13. Haslingfield, Cambridgeshire—Belfry Arch.
14. Grantchester, do. South Doorway.
15. Molding of constant occurrence.
16. St. Alban's.
17. Ryhall, Rutland—Doorway.
18. Do. do. Window.

PLATE X.

1. Diagram of rudimentary Capital.
3. Laceby, Lincolnshire.
4. Middle Rasen, do.
5. Walesby, do.
7. Frieston, do.
8. Do. do.
9. Stickney, do.
10. Do. do.
12. Lincoln Cathedral.
13. Ruskington.
16. Great Abington, Cambridgeshire.
17. Thurlby, Lincolnshire.
18. Furness Abbey, Chapter House.
19. Tintern Abbey.
22. Furness Abbey.
23. Bolton Abbey, Yorkshire.
24. Do. do.
26. Do. do.
28. Tintern Abbey.
29. Arreton, Isle of Wight.
30. Saffron Walden, Essex.
37. Bolton Abbey.
38. Early English Abacus.
39. Decorated Abacus.
40. Early English Capital.

EARLY ENGLISH CAPITALS.

Plate X.

J. H. Le Keux, sc.

PLATE XI.

1. Yaxley, Hunts.
2. Do. do.
3. Fletton, Hunts.
4. Boston, Lincolnshire—Chapel used as Vestry.
6. Leverton, do.
7. Do. do.
9. Sibsey, do.
10. Stickford, do.
11. Partney, do.
12. Legburn, do.
13. Waltham, do.
18. Aswardby, do.
22. Abington, Cambridgeshire.
28. Louth.

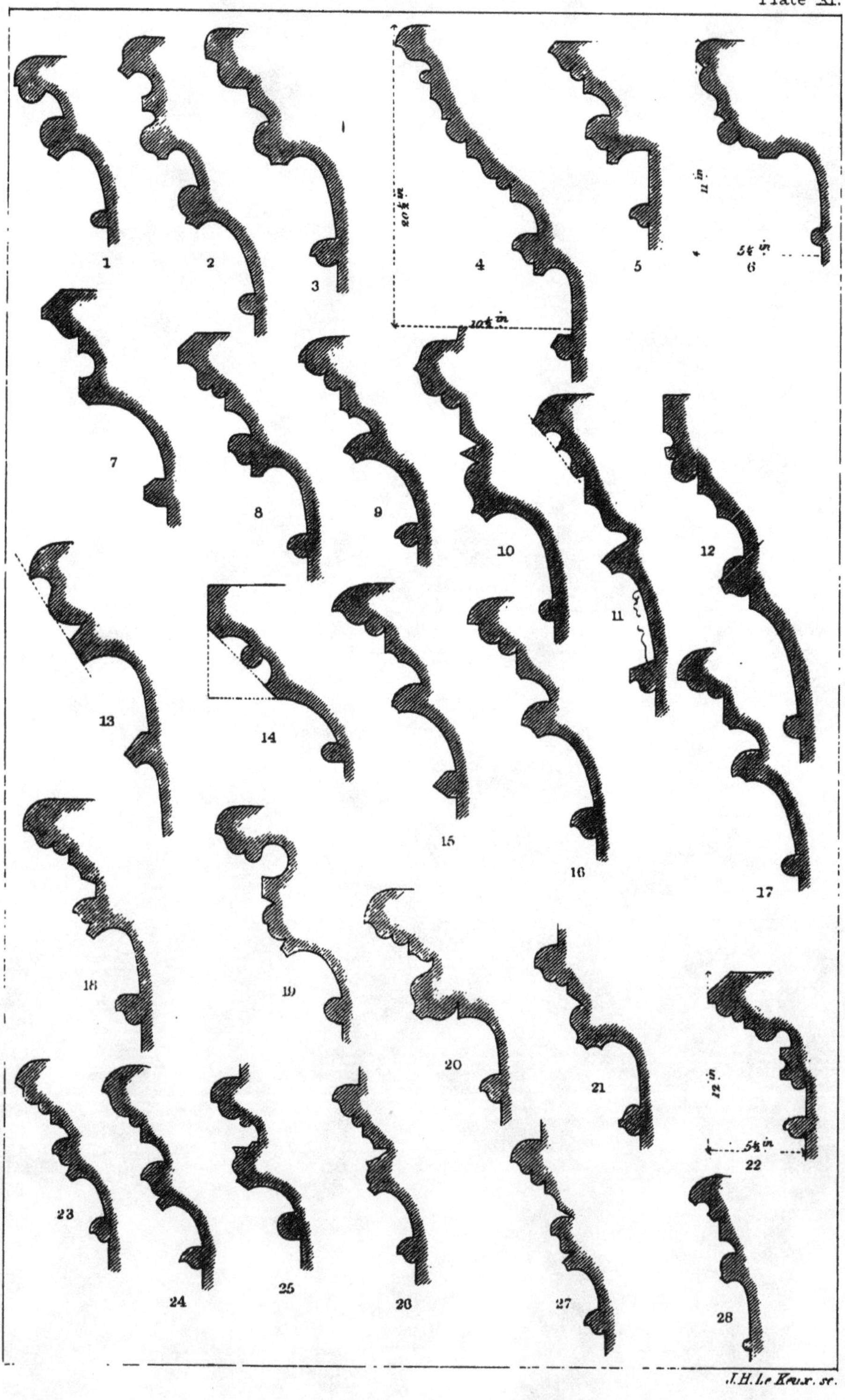
1
2
3
4
5
6
20¼ in
10¼ in
11 in
5¼ in
7
8
9
10
11
12
13
14
15
16
17
18
19
20
21
22
12 in
5¼ in
23
24
25
26
27
28

J.H. Le Keux. sc.

PLATE XII.

11. Trumpington, Cambridgeshire—Capital of Nave Pier.
13. Little Shelford, do. Monument.
14. Maxey, Northamptonshire.
15. Hingham, Norfolk—Nave Piers.
16. Careby, Lincolnshire.
19. Uffington, do.
22. }
23. } St. Martin's, Stamford.
24. }
26. }
27. } St. John's, do.
28. St. George's, do.
29. Bede House, do.

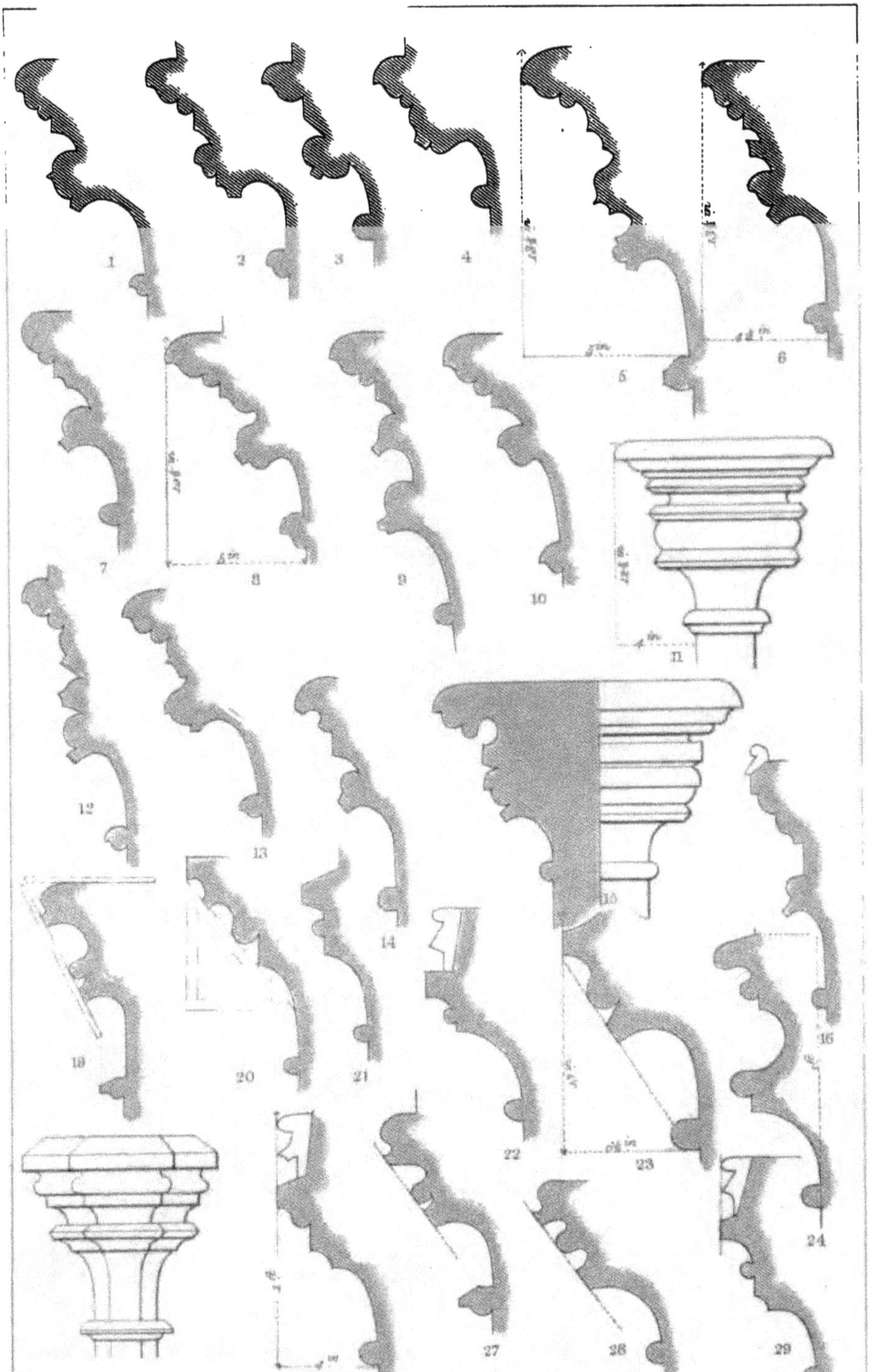

J.H. Le Keux, sc.

PLATE XIII.

1. Long Melford, Suffolk.
4. Louth, Lincolnshire.
8. }
9. } Colchester.
12. }
13. Fen Ditton, Cambridgeshire.
14. Harston, do.
16. Dry Drayton, do.
17. Mattishall, Norfolk.
18. Elsworth Hall, do.
19. Saham Toney, do.

PERPENDICULAR CAPITALS.

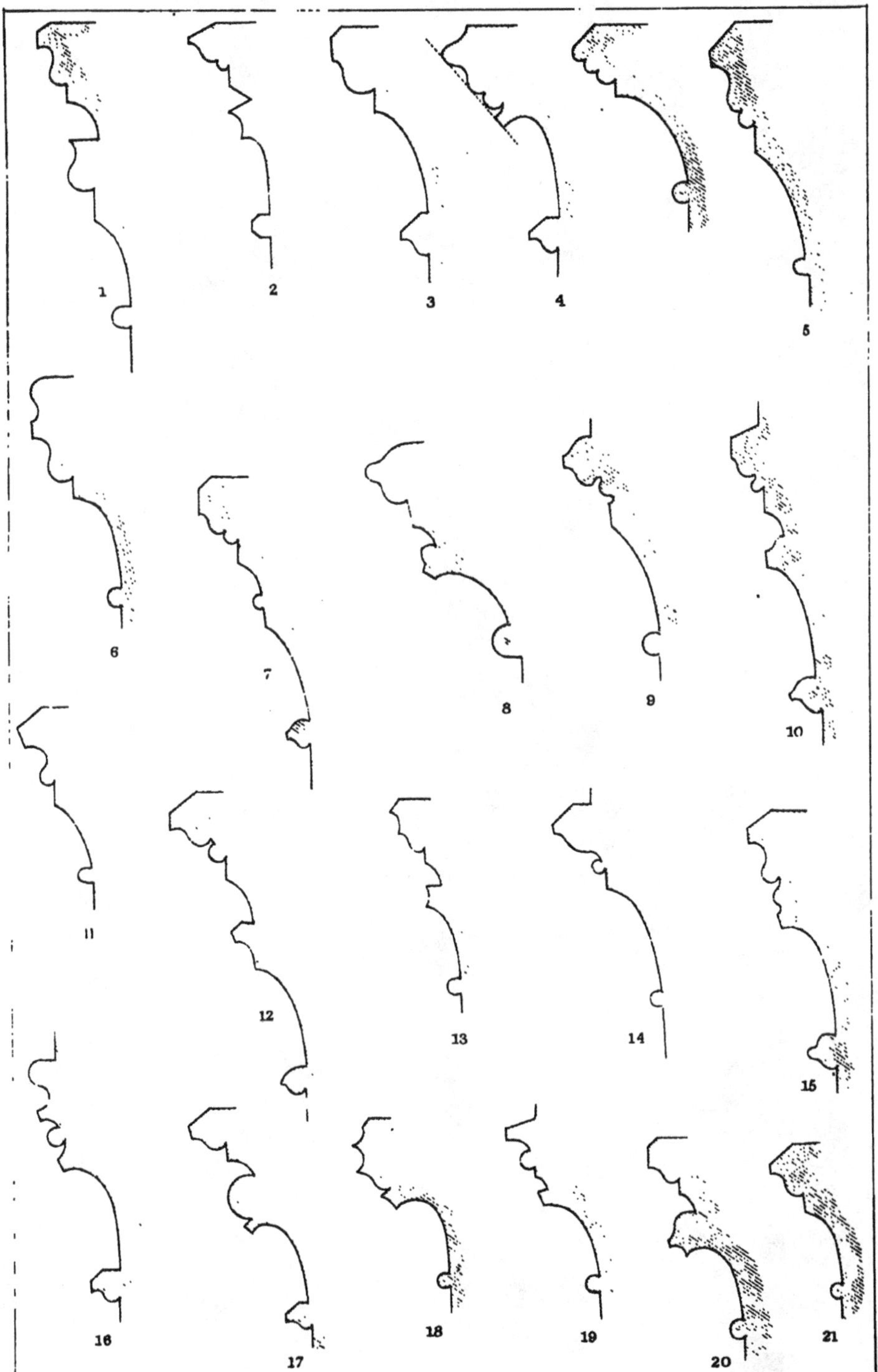

J.H.Le Keux sc.

PLATE XIV.

1. } Attic Base.
2. }
3. } Italian Gothic Bases, from Willis's Architecture of the Middle Ages.
4. }
5. Canterbury Cathedral.
6. Byland Abbey—Central Piers.
7. Peterborough Cathedral.
8. Do. do.
9. Rivaulx Abbey—Choir Columns.
16. Ely Cathedral.
17. Lincoln Cathedral—Base of Great Piers.
18. Do. do.
20. Furness Abbey.
26. Ely Cathedral—Galilee.
27. Skelton, near York.
28. Tintern Abbey.
29. Furness Abbey.
30. Do. do.
33. Tintern Abbey—Nave Piers.
35. Coton, Cambridgeshire.
36. Ely Cathedral—Lady Chapel.
37. St. Mary's Abbey, York.
38. Ely Cathedral—Lady Chapel.
39. Wells Cathedral—Doorway.
40. Do. do. Central Column, Chapter House.
41. Over and Histon, Cambridgeshire.
42. Trumpington—Nave Pier.
43. Bottisham, Cambridgeshire—Nave Piers.
44. Boston, Lincolnshire.
45. Fishtoft, do.

1
2
3
4
5
6
7
8
9
10
11
12
13
14
15
16
17
18
19
20
21
22
23
24
25
26
27
28
29
30
31
32
33
34
35
36
37
38
39
40
41
42
43
44
45
8in
7¼in
22in

J. H. Le Keux, sc

PLATE XV.

1. Crosby Hall.
2. Do. do.
3. Over, Cambridgeshire—Chancel.
4. Peterborough Cathedral—Lady Chapel.
5. Louth.
6. Carbrook, Norfolk.
7. Saham, do.
8. Dereham, do.
9. Norwich Cathedral.
10. Mattishall, Norfolk.
11. Swanton Morley, do.
12. Colchester.
13. All Saints', Stamford.
14. St. John's, do.
15. Colchester.
16. St. Alban's Abbey.
17. Haslingfield, Cambridgeshire.
18. Holy Trinity, Colchester.
20. St. Edward's, Cambridge.
21. Herne, Kent.
22. Saffron Walden, Essex.

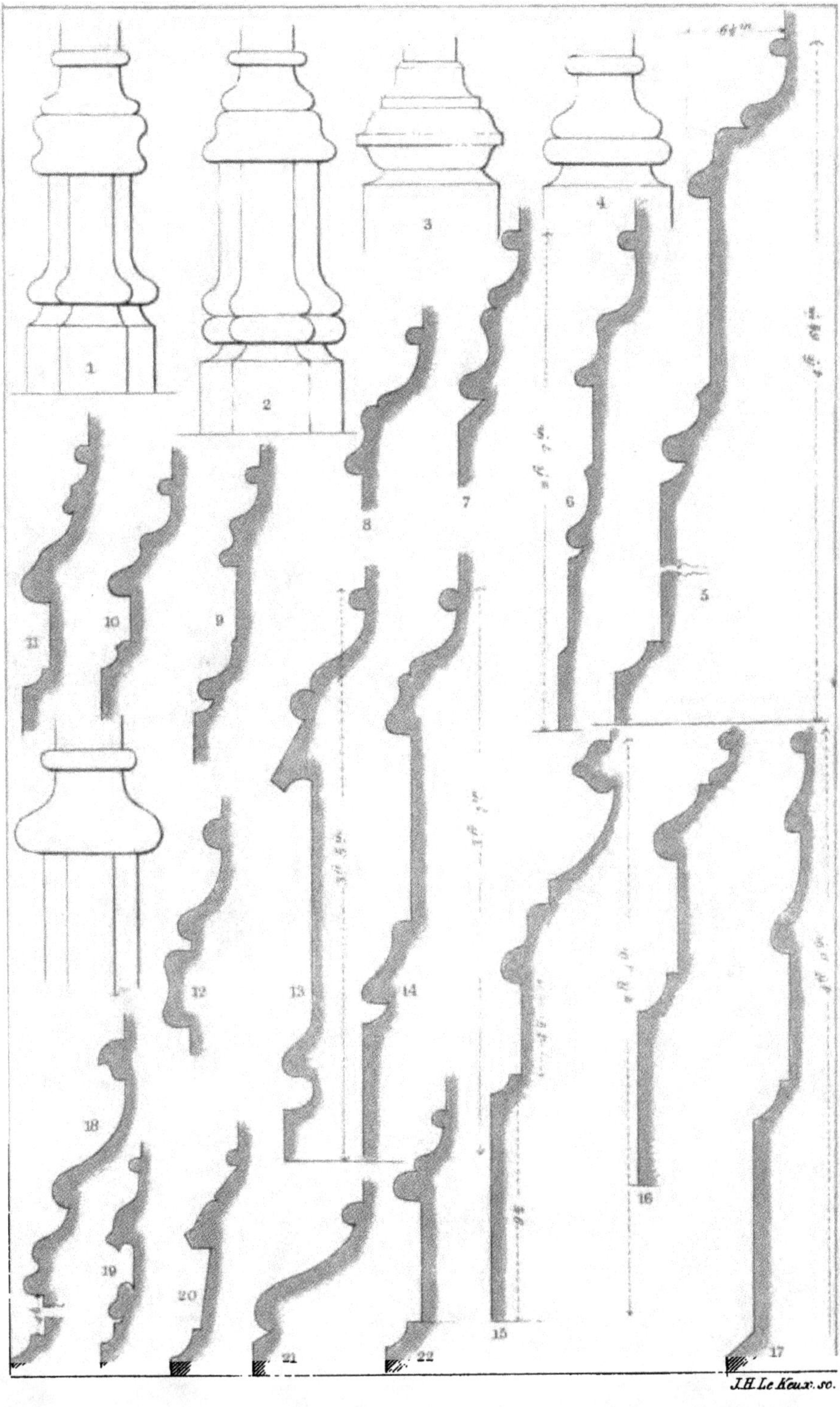

J.H. Le Keux. sc.

PLATE XVI.

Examples of Strings, Hood Molds, &c., from various sources.

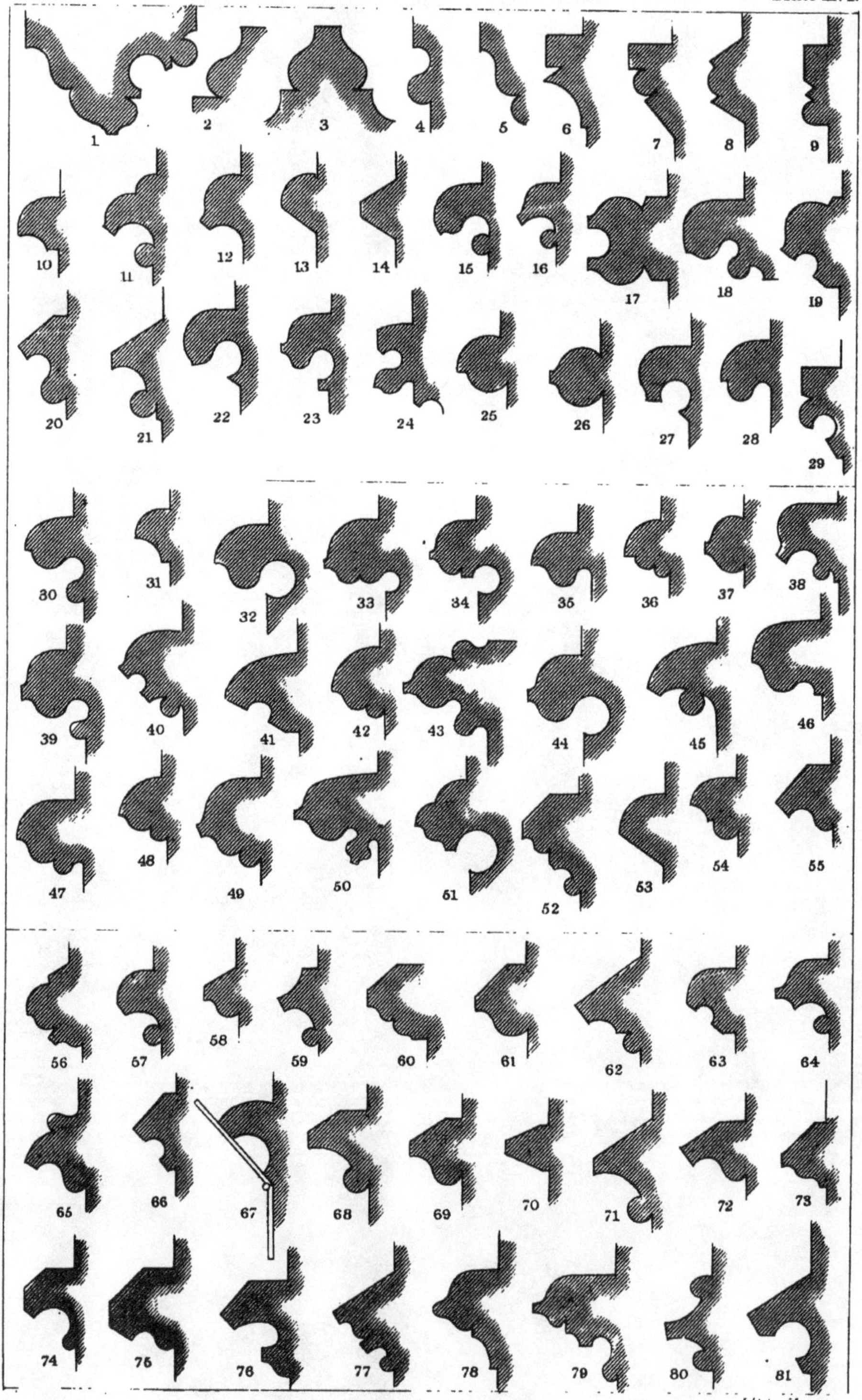
1
2
3
4
5
6
7
8
9
10
11
12
13
14
15
16
17
18
19
20
21
22
23
24
25
26
27
28
29
30
31
32
33
34
35
36
37
38
39
40
41
42
43
44
45
46
47
48
49
50
51
52
53
54
55
56
57
58
59
60
61
62
63
64
65
66
67
68
69
70
71
72
73
74
75
76
77
78
79
80
81

J. H. Le Keux, sc.

PLATE XVII.

1. Bottisham, Cambridgeshire—South Porch.
2. Do. do. North Porch.
3. Do. do. South Porch, Inner Doorway.
4. Grantham, Lincolnshire—South Aisle Window.
5. Langham, Rutland—Doorway.
6. Grantham, Lincolnshire—South Aisle Window.
8. Over, Cambridgeshire—South Porch.
9. Grantham—South Aisle Window.
10. Grantham—Window Jamb.

Plate XVII.

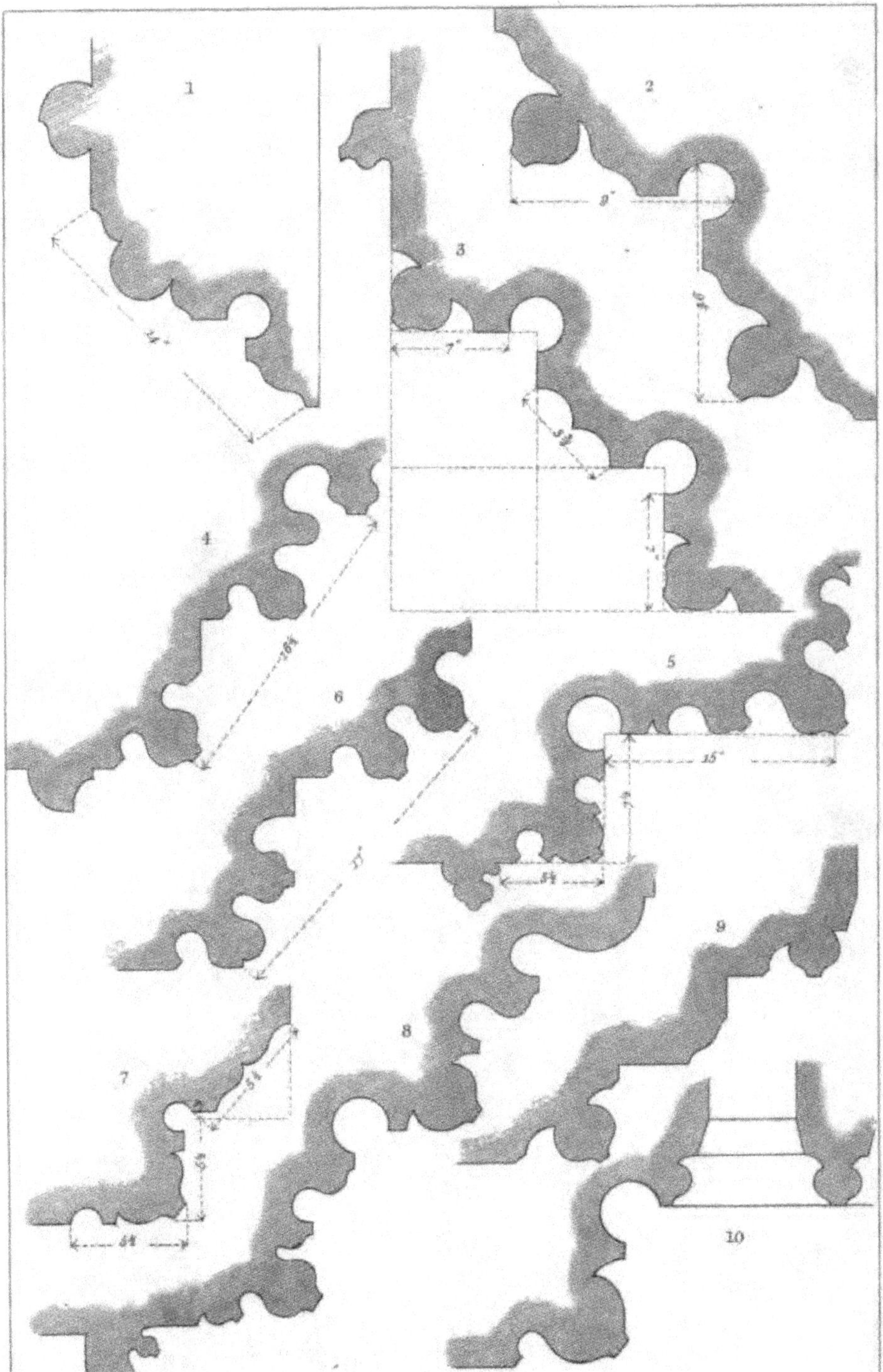

T. Turnbull sc.

PLATE XVIII.

1. Rivaulx Abbey.
2. Peterborough Cathedral—Doorway opposite South Aisle of Nave: half-inch scale.
3. Do. do. Doorway in Cloister: half-inch scale.
4. Rivaulx Abbey—Window Jamb.
5. Do. do. Ruined Doorway.
6. Castle Rising, Norfolk—East Window.
7. Beaulieu Abbey—South Transept Refectory.
8. Ripon Cathedral—Choir.
10. Castle Rising, Norfolk.

Plate XVIII.

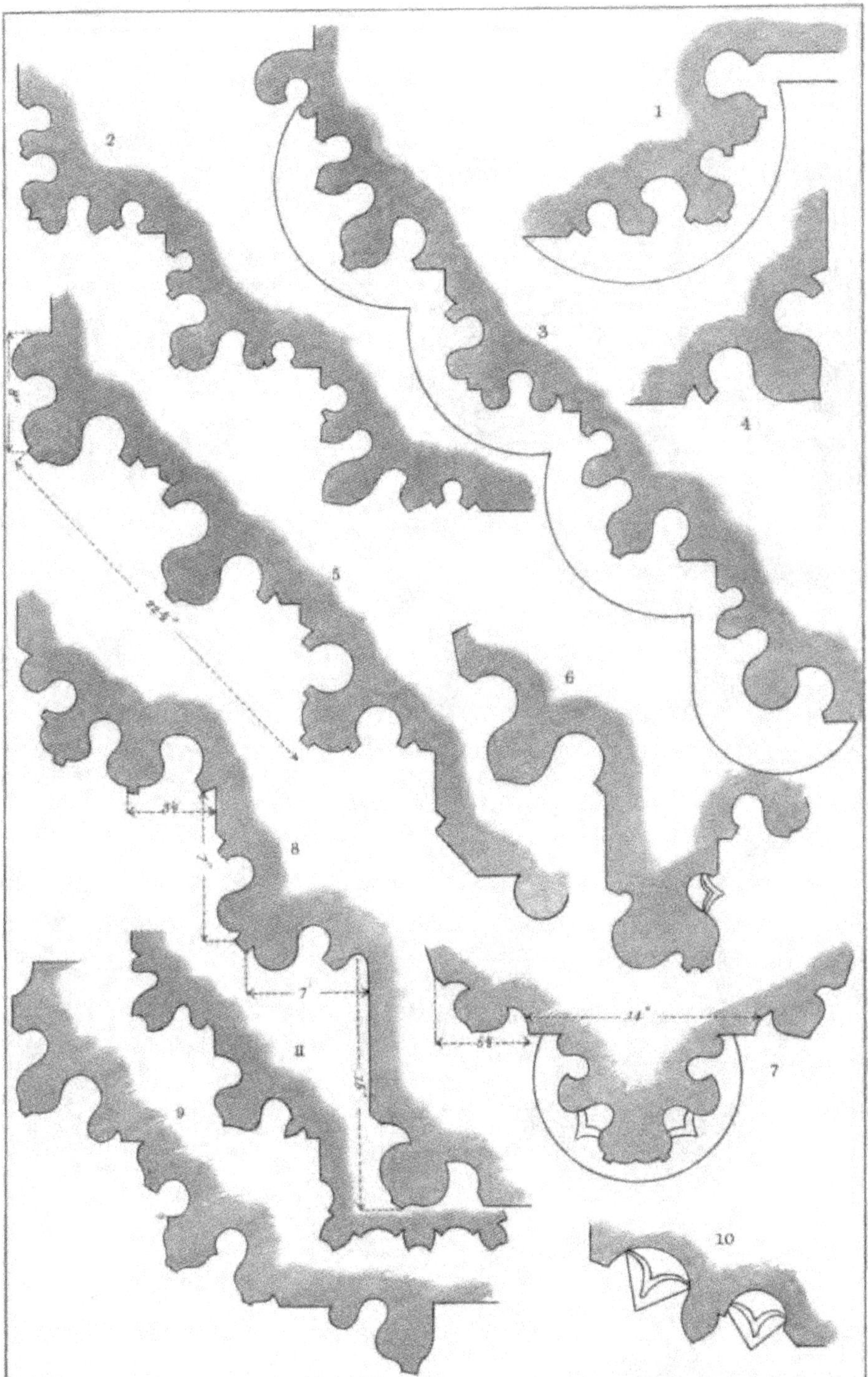

T. Turnbull sc.

Plate XIX.

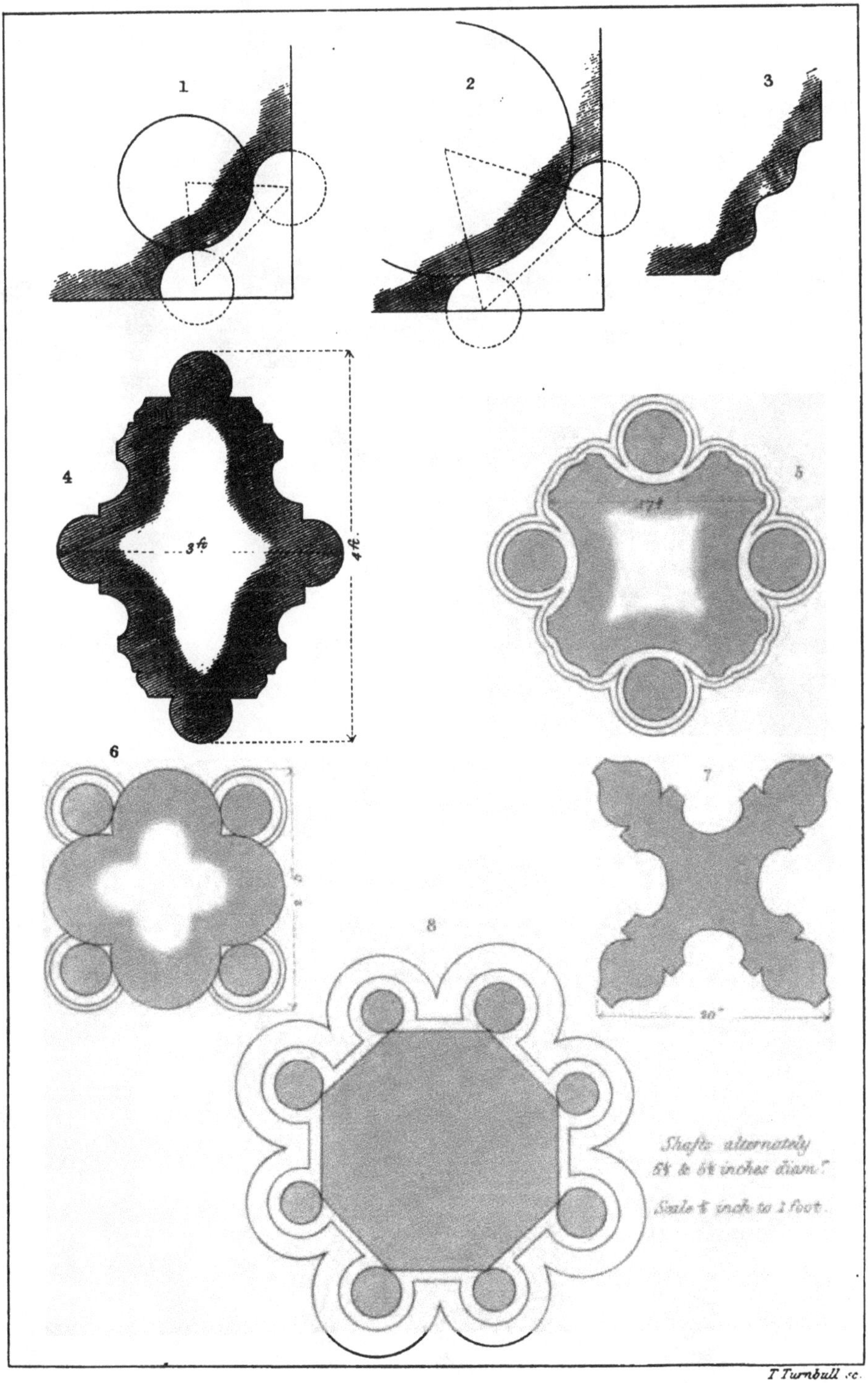

T Turnbull sc.

PLATE XX.

1. Landbeach, Cambridgeshire—Doorway.
2. Quy, do, Window.
3. Grantham—Chancel Window.
4. Peterborough Cathedral—Archway in Cloister.
5. Ripon Cathedral.
6. Rivaulx Abbey.
7. Ripon Cathedral—Window Jamb, South Aisle.
9. Bolton Abbey—Doorway.
10. Newton, near Cambridge—West Doorway.
11. Bolton Abbey.
12. Do. do.
13. Grantham—Choir Doorway.
14. Lancaster—Arch Mold of Nave.
15. Bolton Abbey—Monument.
16. Grantham.
17. Willingham, Cambridgeshire—Chancel Door.
18. Grantham.

Plate XX.

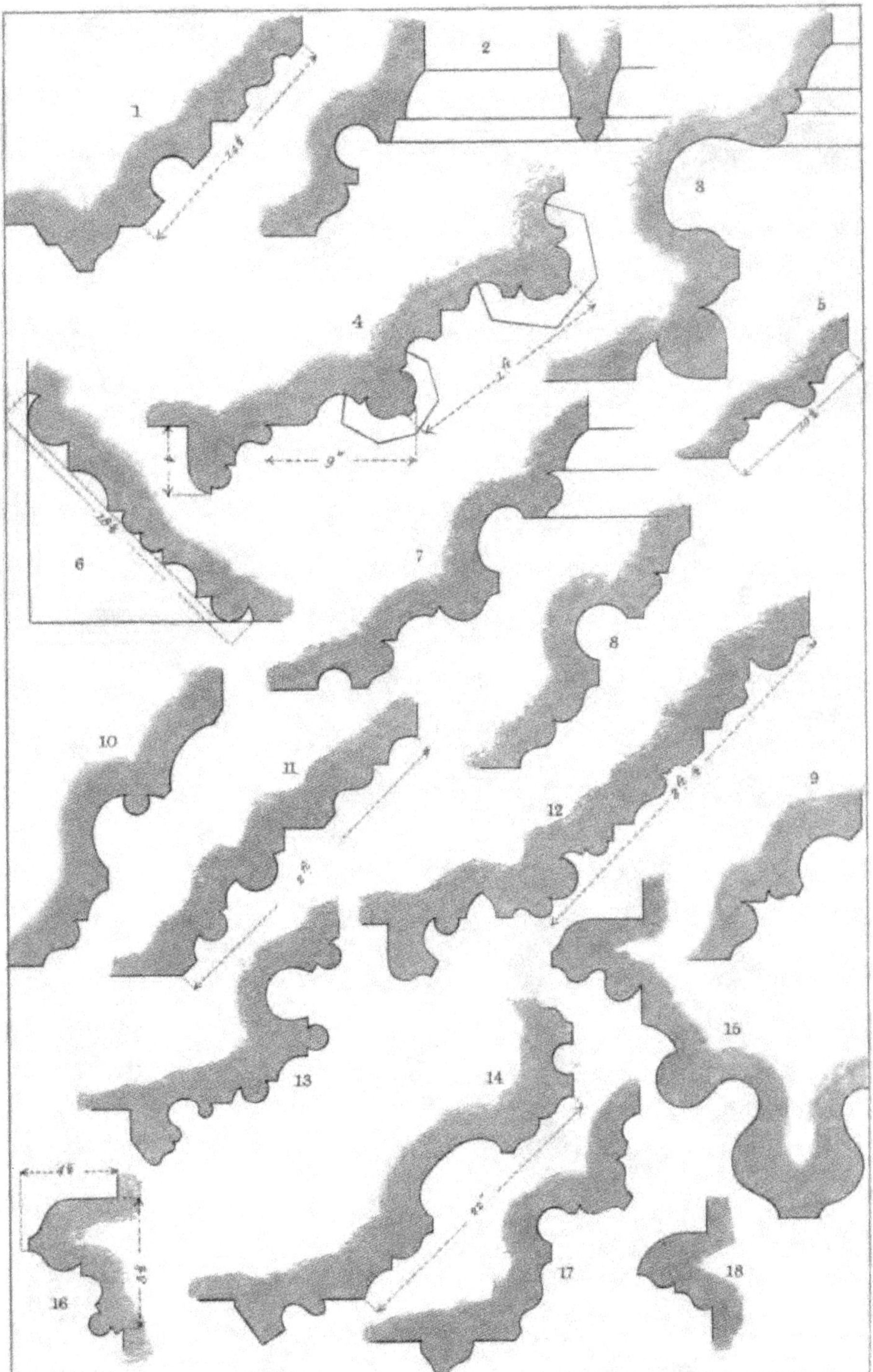

T. Turnbull sc.

PLATE XXI.

1. Morcot, Rutland.
2. Seaton, do.
4. Ripon Cathedral—Revestry or Chapter Room.
5. York Cathedral—Library.
6. Do. do. Nave.
7. Do. do.
8. Ripon Cathedral.
9. Fountains Abbey.
10. Do. do. Chapter House.

Plate XXI.

T. Turnbull sc.

CPSIA information can be obtained
at www.ICGtesting.com
Printed in the USA
LVHW040251230322
714166LV00003B/102

9 783752 586794